To Beatri

Enjoy He

_Ed_

# Journey to the Moon and other stories

Ed Goodwin

*Journey to the Moon and other stories*

Published by The Conrad Press in the United Kingdom 2021

Tel: +44(0)1227 472 874
www.theconradpress.com
info@theconradpress.com

ISBN 978-1-913567-72-9

Copyright © Ed Goodwin, 2021

The moral right of Ed Goodwin to be identified as author of this work has been asserted in accordance with the Copyright, Designs and Patents Act 1988.

All rights reserved.

Typesetting and Cover Design by: Charlotte Mouncey, www.bookstyle.co.uk
Using illustrations from istockphoto.com and Freepik

The Conrad Press logo was designed by Maria Priestley.

Printed and bound in Great Britain by Clays Ltd, Elcograf S.p.A.

# Contents

# Journey to the Moon

# Chapter 1

# The idea

Suzy's life had changed a great deal recently. She had moved to a new house in a village just outside Nottingham. At the same time she had left pre-school and started the first year of 'proper' school. Now she was expected to learn how to read and how to do sums. One of her favourite lessons was when they had to choose what her teacher called a project.

There was a lot of discussion amongst the children and eventually the teacher had drawn up a list for them to choose from.

These included:

Looking after a pet
Learning to bake cup cakes
Doing a magic trick in front of the class

But the project Suzy really wanted to do wasn't in the

list. When Suzy mentioned it in the class the teacher had just laughed and then gone on to discuss one of the other children's ideas.

This idea kept going round and round in Suzy's mind until she could no longer keep it to herself. She knew that if she wanted to do this project Mum would have to agree, because nothing ever happened unless Mum approved.

One evening when Suzy had got back from school she decided the time was right to tell Mum about her idea.

'Mum,' she said.

'Yes?'

'I want to go to the moon.'

Her mum who was used to such things just continued heating up the spaghetti hoops.

'I really want to go to the moon,' said Suzy.

'Maybe when you're a bit older,' said Mum.

'No, I want to go tonight,' insisted Suzy.

'Well you have to have your tea now.'

Suzy and her younger sister Connie sat down and ate their spaghetti hoops followed by yoghurts.

The moon idea had been forgotten Mum thought.

Ten minutes later Dad got back from work.

'How did you get on at school today?' he asked Suzy.

'I want to go to the moon,' she replied.

'And me too,' said Connie.

'That sounds like a good idea to me,' said Dad who often had some weird ideas himself.

'Oh no!' thought Mum.

'But we have to go to Suzy's swimming lesson first,' said Dad.

The girls then started chanting, 'We want to go the moon, we want to go to the moon, we want to go to the moon.'

This lasted for the next five minutes, before Suzy was persuaded to get into her swimming costume and then to be taken to her lesson.

The next day it was Dad's turn to look after the girls after school. He was cooking fish fingers and beans when Suzy came into the kitchen.

'Please Dad can we go to the moon, Mummy said we could?'

Now while Dad knew this wasn't true, he still thought it might be a good idea.

'OK,' he said. 'But we need to find out how to do it,

we'll go to the library on Saturday, and find a book to help us.'

Meanwhile Connie was playing in the lounge with her toy monkey repeating, 'Go to the moon, go to the moon, go to the moon.'

Saturday came round and Dad had to live up to his promise and go to the library with Suzy.

'Have you got any books about going to the moon?' Suzy asked the librarian.

'Why, are you going there?' the librarian laughed. Suzy didn't find this funny.

'Over there there're some books about the planets.'

As Suzy had only just started to read, Dad read out the title of the books there were *Children's guide to the Planets, History of the Moon, The Story of the Solar System* but none of these explained how to get to the moon and besides they didn't have many pictures.

They were just going to give up when on the bottom shelf Dad spotted the book they had been looking for: *Young Girls' Guide to Going to the Moon.* The journey was about to begin.

# Chapter 2

# The discussion

When they got back home Mum, Dad, Suzy and Connie started looking at the book. Suzy had lots of questions.

'When can we go?'

'Can we take Connie if she's only three?'

'How long will it take to get there?'

'Will we get back before my birthday?'

After what seemed like hours of questions Dad was beginning to go off the idea and Mum who thought it was a bad idea in the first place had gone out for a run. Meanwhile Dad had been thinking about more practical things.

How to make a rocket?

How to make the clothes to keep them safe in the rocket?

What food to take with them?

How much would it all cost?

Later that evening after the children had gone to bed Mum and Dad had a discussion.

'Look, this is a stupid idea,' said Mum. 'She can't really go to the moon. There's never been any children gone there before.'

'Why not?' said Dad. 'I can make a rocket at work.'

'Not big enough to go to the moon. That would cost millions of pounds.'

'We could do a sponsored bike ride to raise the money.'

'No we couldn't. You'll have to tell Suzy she can't go.'

'I can't do that. You know what she's like, she'll never give up on the idea, and Connie wants to go now.'

'Well that's your problem. You'll have to think of a way to let her down gently.'

That night Dad couldn't get to sleep. How would he tell Suzy the moon trip was cancelled?

# Chapter 3

# Dad makes a decision

The following day Dad woke up early at half past six. He was feeling all right because he had decided what to do, how to tell Suzy the moon trip was cancelled. He went to make a cup of tea for himself and Mum and returned to the bedroom.

After he had had his drink he could hear Suzy and Connie playing in the living room. He took a deep breath and went in to see them. Connie was running round the room with a toy plane in her hand shouting 'Let's fly to the moon,' while Suzy was reading *Young Girls' Guide to Going to the Moon.*

'I've got something to tell you,' he said.

'Yes,' said Suzy and Connie together.

'Oh never mind,' said Dad.

'I thought you were going to tell us when we are going to the moon,' Suzy said. 'When are we going to go? I've read the book now so I know what we have to do. When are we going to go?'

'Go and ask Mum,' Dad said.

The girls ran into the bedroom.

'Mum, Mum, when are we going?'

'Going where?' said Mum

'To the moon, of course,' Suzy said.

'Hasn't Dad told you?' Mum said, already guessing at the answer.

'No he said ask you,' Suzy replied.

'Dave!' Mum shouted. 'Come here!'

Dad rather slowly made his way into the bedroom.

'I thought you were going to tell them.'

'I just couldn't do it they were so excited,' said Dad.

This is typical, thought Mum.

'OK girls, I'm afraid you can't go to the moon.'

'Why?' the girls chorused.

'Because it costs too much money,' tried Mum.

'Why?' said Connie.

'Well you have to buy all the petrol for the rocket and then you have to build it.'

'Why?' said Connie.

'Just stop saying why,' Mum said. 'You're not going. Now let's get you ready for school.'

The girls trooped out into their bedrooms with their chins slumped on their chests.

'I know what to do,' said Suzy to Connie.

They went down to the lounge and Suzy opened *Young Girls' Guide to Going to the Moon*.

She could read it quite well. Chapter 3 was called *What to do when mum says no.*

She turned the pages to get to that chapter, it was very short, it said Ask Dad.

Chapter 4 was called *What to do when dad says no.*

In it were lots of things to do to get your own way Suzy and Connie started planning what they could do.

# Getting the right answer

'Look Connie the book tells us what to do,' Suzy said.

'You read it to me,' said Connie.

'OK but then you have to remember to do all the things it says.'

'I'm ready,' said Connie.

Suzy began.

'Always look sad.'

'Take longer than normal to get dressed.'

'Keep putting your shoes on the wrong feet.'

'Put your coat on inside out.'

'Refuse to eat your dinner, but not for too long otherwise you'll get hungry.'

'Refuse to eat anything except ham sandwiches and ice cream, for all meals including breakfast.'

'Keep asking why we can't go to the moon, at least fifty times a day.'

'The book says after a week most mums and dads will give up and let you go,' Suzy said.

The girls started following the advice by looking sad. Connie was brilliant at this but neither Mum nor Dad seemed to notice anything different.

Worse, they were allowed to go to school or in Connie's case pre-school with their shoes on the wrong feet and their coats inside out. Mum and Dad just didn't seem to mind but their school friends all laughed at them.

After two weeks they were getting fed up of eating ham sandwiches and ice cream all the time.

Suzy started to wonder if the advice in *Young Girls' Guide to Going to the Moon* was correct. When on the third week after Connie had asked for the three hundred and seventieth time, 'Why can't we go to the moon?' Dad finally caved in using a word Suzy had never heard before and not since. The girls knew their journey was really going to happen.

## Chapter 5

# A mystery

That night Dad couldn't get to sleep; He knew he shouldn't have given in and had no idea what to do next.

Mum also was awake but her mind was churning away. Finally she said 'I've got an idea.'

'Yeees,' said Dad sleepily.

'We need to see what the guide says. Surely it can't say they have to go in a real space rocket from America.'

'Well probably not,' yawned Dad.

'We need to get the book off Suzy,' said Mum.

'That will be difficult,' replied Dad. 'She sleeps with it under her pillow and keeps hold of it all the time.'

'Why can't we just ask her for it?'

'I don't want her to think we'll do what the book says before I've had a look,' said Mum.

'I can see if the library has another copy,' said Dad.

'Or maybe buy one from eBay,' said Mum.

Next morning after the girls had been taken to school, Suzy carrying the guide tucked under her arm, Dad set off to the library. When he got there he saw the same librarian he had seen a few weeks ago.

'Hello,' he said

'Hi,' she replied.

'I borrowed a book for my daughter a few weeks ago called *Young Girls' Guide to Going to the Moon* . I wondered if you had another copy.'

'Why?' replied the librarian sharply. 'Most people only borrow one copy of a book, why do you want two?'

Dad thought quickly. 'Her sister wants one as well,' he lied.

'All right,' the librarian said. 'Let me have a look.' There was nothing on the bookshelves so she signed on to the computer, quickly hit a lot of keys and then sat back staring at the screen.

'We don't have a book with that title,' she said.

'Don't you have a record of it being borrowed?' Dad said. 'It was for Suzy Goodwin.'

'No nothing,' the librarian replied.

'In fact there's no record of a book ever being written

with that title.'

'That can't be right. Can you check again?'

The librarian was getting a bit fed up but went to check anyway.

'No, definitely no book with that title has ever been written.'

Dad had also looked on his smartphone and couldn't find a book with that title either.

'I might be back. I'm sure that was the title,' he said uncertainly as he walked out of the library.

# Chapter 6

# The book disappears

Dad went back to his office, but he couldn't stop thinking about the book. Why didn't the librarian know about it? Why was there no record of it on the internet? How had it got into the library? Was it magical?

When he got home that evening he had to tell Mum about it straightaway.

'You might think this is a bit strange,' he began.

'Oh,' said Mum.

'Well you know I went into the library to get another copy of the guide. Well they said they didn't have one, in fact they had never had a book titled *Young Girls' Guide to Going to the Moon* and that no such book existed.'

'Are you joking?' said Mum as Dad quite often made up stories which weren't true.

Dad looked as serious as he could manage. 'No it's absolutely true. I even checked on my smartphone and there's nothing about the guide there either.'

'But we've got it here haven't we? Let's ask Suzy if we can have a look. Maybe it will say who wrote it.'

'Suzy can we have a look at the guide?' Mum asked.

'Which guide?' said Suzy pretending she didn't know what Mum meant.

'*The* guide. The guide to going to the moon.'

Suzy put down the puppet she had been playing with and went to get it from her sandwich box.

It wasn't there!

'I've lost it,' said Suzy who didn't seem at all bothered and went back to playing with her puppet.

'Aren't you going to have a look for it? You don't seem very worried,' Mum said.

'It's OK I've lost it a few times, it just disappears but at bedtime it's always under my pillow.'

'Have a look and see if it's there now.' Suzy did as she was told and went upstairs to have a look under her pillow. Connie went to have a look under *her* pillow just to join in although it had never been there. But it wasn't under Suzy's pillow and of course not under Connie's.

'Mum, it's not there,' Suzy said. 'We'll just have to

wait till later. It always reappears just like magic.'

Mum and Dad looked at each other but didn't say anything but they were beginning to think it could be magical.

A few hours passed and it was time for the girls to go to bed. Dad had just finished reading the Gruffalo book for what seemed the hundredth time and the girls were both in bed.

With mounting excitement Dad said 'Can I have a look at the guide now?' 'What guide?' said Suzy.

'Don't start that again, you know what guide,' said Dad. Suzy lifted up her pillow but it wasn't there. Dad stared at the empty space and suddenly it *was* there. He went to pick it up but it wasn't there anymore, had he just imagined it?

'It it's gone,' he stuttered. 'Well sometimes it's not there at night but it's there in the morning it's like the tooth fairy,' Suzy said.

'Yes but that's really Mum or,' he stopped just in time . 'I'll have a look at it when you get up tomorrow. Goodnight girls.'

'Daddy can the tooth fairy leave me some money

tonight?' said Connie.

'Have you lost a tooth today ?' said Dad.

'I don't think so,' said Connie.

'She'll be going to see another girl tonight,' said Dad and with that closed the bedroom door.

'Well,' said Mum. 'What happened?' Mum and Dad were relaxing with a cup of tea in the kitchen. 'I'm not sure,' said Dad. 'The guide wasn't under the pillow then it was, then it wasn't again.'

Mum look a bit doubtful. 'That is what happened, honest,' said Dad. 'We'll both go and have a look tomorrow morning.'

It was going to be another sleepless night in the Goodwin household.

# Chapter 7

# The book reappears

Next morning Mum and Dad had both got up early at six, and made their way quietly into the girls' bedroom. Connie was fast asleep and Suzy was snoring, with her head on the pillow. Mum and Dad sat on the floor by the side of her bed waiting for Suzy to wake up.

Half an hour later Suzy woke up, lazily stretched her arms towards the ceiling and then shrieked 'eeeeee' as she saw two faces a few inches away from her face. This woke Connie up who started crying.

'Sorry darling,' said Mum. 'We just want to check if the guide is under your pillow.' Suzy would have said 'What guide?' if she had been more awake but instead sat up straight and reached under her pillow and gave the book to Dad.

The book felt a bit cold but there was no doubt it was the same book as before. He looked at the cover to see who had written it.

'There isn't an author,' he said to Mum. 'But look what's written in the preface.' Suzy didn't know what they were talking about.

'Why isn't there an otter, and why has the book got a face?'

Mum sighed 'It's an author not otter, an author is the person who wrote the book.'

' And the author (Suzy said this word slowly) hasn't got a face?'

'It's nothing to do with a face,' Mum said. 'It's preface and it's the introduction to the book.'

'What does the preface say then?'

' It says you are not the only owner of this book.'

Connie had stopped crying and was as usual trying to join in a conversation she didn't understand. 'It belongs to my unicorn,' she said in a very serious voice.

'No I don't think so,' said Dad.

'Yes it does,' said Connie defiantly.

'But Dad it's mine,' said Suzy.

'Let's leave it for now,' Mum said trying to calm things down.

'But it *is* mine,' whined Suzy.

'Yes,' said Dad. ' Now let's get you up and dressed.'

The book was soon forgotten as the girls had their breakfast and got their school bags ready. They jumped up into Mum's car, Suzy with the guide tucked under her arm.

'We'll read it this evening,' whispered Mum to Dad. 'Then we can make a plan, we won't have to do everything the guide says.'

'That's if it hasn't disappeared by then,' Dad replied frowning.

Chapter 8

# The Plan

That evening the girls asked about going to the moon again.

'If you're going to the moon we need to read the book and make a plan,' said Dad.

Mum's jaw dropped it was so unusual for Dad to suggest making a plan let alone following any instructions.

'Can you get the book,' he said to Suzy.

'What book?' said Suzy. But when Dad gave her one of his sternest looks she hurried off to get the guide from her sandwich box.

Brushing the crumbs off Dad opened the book at the chapter *Making the Rocket.*

'I'll tell you what,' said Mum. 'We'll write down the plan on the whiteboard.' She took it down from the wall and started to write down the things to do. After about

two hours of arguments, after which Suzy had finally
agreed to take only ten soft toys the list looked like this.

Build Rocket – Dad Suzy and Connie

Pack clothes for a week – Mum

Make space suits - Dad

Check walkie-talkies are working – Mum, Suzy

Take books to read – Suzy and Connie

Pack vitamin tablets – Mum

Take fifty bottles of water – Mum

Decide when to go – Mum

(Suzy and Connie wanted to go tomorrow, but Mum
had gently suggested they would have to wait a bit longer
and it was finally agreed that Mum would decide.)

When it came to the space suit design Dad had
ignored what the guide said and come up with his own,
rather cool he thought, list of materials.

Snow White dress, swimming goggles, wellingtons,
saucepan (with eyeholes and mouth holes), mittens,
oxygen tank.

In the guide it warned that building the rocket
could take a few weeks but here again Dad had an
idea for a much simpler design. This mainly involved

using cardboard boxes, crayons, Sellotape, and an old lawnmower engine.

'Is there anything else in the guide?' asked Mum.

'Well there is the chapter *What to do when things go wrong* but I don't think we need to bother too much about that,' said Dad. (Would that be a bad decision?)

Mum and Dad had been so engrossed in making the plan that they hadn't noticed that Suzy and Connie were sleeping face down on the floor. Gently they lifted them up and put them to bed without waking them.

Mum went downstairs to fetch the book and put it under Suzy's pillow but it had disappeared again. 'Oh well,' she thought. 'It will probably be back tomorrow.'

# Chapter 9

# Preparation part one

The next few days saw plenty of activity. Dad dismantling the lawn mower and drilling holes in saucepans. 'Shouldn't you have checked the saucepans were big enough to go over their heads before drilling the holes?' Mum asked.

'Oh yes,' said Dad who was swiftly despatched to the supermarket to buy some new ones.

Meanwhile Mum had smuggled two oxygen cylinders out of the hospital where she worked, the girls had started crayoning stars on the side of some cardboard boxes and Mum and Suzy had started to test out the walkie-talkies.

'Will they work?' said Dad. 'I thought you couldn't hear each other if you were more than two miles apart, and it's about 240,000 miles from earth to the moon'.

Dad had done some research on the internet to try

and make up for the saucepans disaster.

'The guide says they will work,' said Suzy and that stopped any further discussion.

'Mum to Suzy,' Mum spoke into the walkie-talkie. She was in the kitchen and Suzy was in the bedroom upstairs, nothing happened.

'What's wrong?' she shouted.

'You forgot to say over,' shouted Suzy.

Mum tried again 'Can you hear me over?'

Still nothing. Mum realised she had forgotten to press the button. ' I'll try again,' she shouted.

Pressing the button she said 'Hello Suzy over,' still no reply.

'I did everything right that time,' she shouted.

'I just went for a wee,' Suzy shouted back.

Mum decided they would try again later.

After one week Mum thought it was a good idea to see how far everyone had got with their jobs. First Connie demonstrated the rocket. It was like a cardboard snake stretching from the living room to the downstairs bathroom. Connie and Suzy could stand up inside but it was very dark because there weren't any windows.

'Why does it go into the bathroom?' Dad asked.

'It's so we can go to the toilet and have a bath during the flight,' explained Suzy. This seemed a good idea to everybody.

Next it was Dad's turn to show the space suits. Suzy and Connie put on their Snow White dresses then Dad helped them to put on their wellingtons, and mittens and swimming goggles. Mum tied the oxygen cylinders on their backs with some string. By this time Suzy and Connie were finding it difficult to stand up. Finally Dad brought the saucepans over and placed them over their heads.

'I can't see anything!' cried Connie.

'I can't either!' exclaimed Suzy. Dad had made a mistake in his measurements and would have to buy some more saucepans.

'Let's have another try next weekend,' said Mum, exchanging an angry glance with Dad.

Chapter 10

# Preparation part two

Next Friday after Suzy had come back from school Mum decided to have another meeting. Connie once again demonstrated the progress on the space ship. It now had two windows and also a door. 'Look Mum, we've put in two sleeping bags'. Mum was pleased to see that, but wasn't too happy about them being stapled to the living room carpet.

'That's so they don't move when there's no gravity,' Dad said. Now Suzy knew all about gravity because she had watched a TV programme about it. But not for the first time Connie didn't understand, and just continued to show the other parts of the rocket.

'Here's the engine,' she said.

'I expected you to remove the engine from the lawnmower,' Mum said to Dad.

'I thought it best to keep it altogether,' Dad replied.

'It's so you can start it by pressing the switch on the handle.'

Connie walked over to one of the windows.

'Our clothes are here,' she pointed to a small wooden box, also stapled to the carpet. 'And here are our toys,' she said pointing to the bedside cabinet next to it.

'Where's your food?' Mum asked.

'Daddy's going to make it all.'

'Yes that's why I bought ten loaves of bread,' Dad said. 'It won't take long for me to make 200 cheese sandwiches.'

Rather worriedly Mum asked Dad 'How are the spacesuits?'

'I'll show you.' The girls changed into their Snow White dresses, wellingtons, mittens, saucepans. 'They all fit now,' said Suzy.

'What about the oxygen cylinders?' said Mum.

'It's all right we decided not to take them,' said Dad.

'What!' shouted Mum.

'The book said you don't need them, you can just fill balloons with the oxygen and burst them when you need them.'

'And just how many balloons do you need for that?' Mum's voice was getting higher.

'Er about 200,' said Dad. 'It won't take long for me to fill them. I can use the pump we use to blow up the travel mattress.'

'It seems to me you're not ready yet.' said Mum. 'Let's check everything next weekend.'

'Aww,' chorused the girls , and Dad.

'I mean it,' said Mum.

Would they be ready to go next Friday?

# Chapter 11

## Blast off

Next Wednesday Mum and Dad sat down to have a serious conversation.

'If the rocket is ready next Friday the girls will want to go,' started Mum.

'Well that's OK it will just be like a sleepover, they will go into the rocket on Friday and when they wake up they will come out. We can decorate the living room with cotton wool on the floor and pictures of stars on the wall to pretend it's the moon.'

'So you don't think it's real then, they won't really go to the moon?' said Mum.

'Of course not,' said Dad.

'So why have you just made 200 cheese sandwiches, as well as ruining my carpet ?' Mum asked. Dad couldn't think of a good reply.

'Do *you* think it's real?' he asked.

'I don't know,' said Mum. 'It sounds ridiculous, but then there's this thing with the guide that keeps disappearing and reappearing that's ridiculous as well.'

'We have to let them think they're going to the moon,' said Dad. 'I can't stand another two weeks of them asking why they can't go.'

'I suppose so,' said Mum shrugging her shoulders. 'I'll check everything on Friday and if it's all right then we can let them into the rocket when it gets dark. When it seems they've gone to sleep we'll decorate the living room. They can wake up in the morning then get out and pretend they're on the moon.'

'Yes , I think that will work,' said Dad.

I hope so, thought Mum.

Friday evening came and the girls were beside themselves with excitement. Connie could hardly eat any tea, and Suzy was reading out parts of the guide which explained what it would be like on the moon.

'Let me check the rocket again,' said Mum.

All the sandwiches were neatly stacked in plastic boxes, together with the water. Balloons were floating about everywhere. Dad had put some curtains over the windows and also brought in two torches. He seemed to have thought of everything.

'It seems OK to me,' said Mum. 'Well done!'

'Did you bring the walkie-talkies?' Dad asked Suzy.

'Oh, I forgot,' said Suzy. 'They're in our bedroom'. Connie and Suzy went off to look for them. They returned after two minutes. 'We can't find them,' said Suzy. Mum went to have a look and came back a minute later.

'You didn't look very well,' she said. 'They were on your bed.'

Mum gave one of the walkie-talkies to Suzy, keeping one for herself.

'I want one,' said Connie.

'We only have two,' said Dad calmly, 'and Mum has to have one of them.' Connie responded by slumping down on the floor crying and refusing to move. Suzy put her arm round her.

'You can share it with me,' she said softly.

'No I want my own,' cried Connie.

'I think you're going to have to buy another one,' said Mum to Dad.

'They only sell them in twos,' said Dad .

'Well get two then.'

Dad had to go to the toy shop and buy the walkie-talkies. He gave one to Connie who stopped crying immediately.

It had now become dark outside.

'Get into your pj's,' said Dad. The girls had never got ready for bed so quickly. They came downstairs and stood upright outside the rocket. They gave Mum and Dad a hug. 'Go into the rocket now,' said Dad.

Once inside it was very dark and the girls kept bumping into the balloons.

'Make yourself comfortable,' Mum said. 'Then shut the door. I'm starting the countdown now, ten, nine, eight, seven, six, five, four, three, two, one, blast off.'

# Chapter 12

# The journey part one

Mum and Dad couldn't hear any noise from the rocket so they started putting out the cotton wool around it and pictures of stars Blu-Tacked to the walls.

The local supermarket had become a bit suspicious of Dad's shopping habits recently.

When on top of the unusual number of saucepans, loaves of bread , and huge amounts of cheese he had recently bought he then went back to buy a hundred packs of cotton wool they were thinking of reporting him to the police but couldn't quite think of a good enough reason.

After decorating the living room Mum and Dad went to bed planning to wake up early next morning and take part in pretending to be on the moon with the girls.

Inside the rocket after the words 'blast off' Suzy had remembered what she had to do. 'Switch on the

lawnmower,' she said to herself. 'Then leave it on till
I count to one hundred.' Suzy and Connie started
counting one, two, three, … ninety-nine, one hundred.
'Now turn it off.' It had become very dark inside the
rocket. And she had also started to float so it was not
easy to turn it off, but with Connie holding her steady
she managed to do it 'Then burst a few balloons,' she
continued. That bit was frightening Suzy didn't like loud
noises, but she burst them very quickly with a pin.

'This is fun,' said Connie using swimming strokes
to float around the inside of the rocket. Twisting and
turning to avoid bumping into the balloons. Meanwhile
Suzy was practising cartwheels, which were much easier
to do now in the air.

After all the floating around the girls became very tired
and decided to snuggle into their sleeping bags. They
hadn't looked out of the windows so hadn't noticed how
black it was outside or the very bright stars.

Mum and Dad woke up early on the Saturday
morning. 'I can't hear anything from the living room,'
said Dad.

'No I can't either,' said Mum. 'Let's walk downstairs

quietly and see what's going on.'

They crept downstairs into the living room and then stared around them shocked by what they could see. The rocket had gone leaving behind some holes in the carpet. The girls were nowhere to be seen.

'They must have taken it outside or into the garage,' said Mum. They looked around everywhere but couldn't find the girls or the rocket.

'Where can they have gone?' said Dad.

'I know,' said Mum. 'I can try the walkie-talkie.' She went into the kitchen to get one of them. 'Suzy it's Mum where are you?' No answer.

'You forgot to say over.' Dad reminded her.

'OK,' said Mum. 'Mum to Suzy where are you over?'

There was a crackling sound then a faint voice 'I'm in the rocket we're in space,' said Suzy.

'Are you hiding somewhere over?'

'No we actually are in space over.'

'How do you know, over?'

'We can see a black sky and stars outside and the moon is bigger than normal over.'

'Where's Connie over?'

'She's just by me she can talk on her own walkie-talkie.'

Mum rushed in the kitchen to get the other walkie-talkie.

'Connie over.'

'Hello Mummy.' (Connie was not so good at remembering to say over).

'Where are you over?'

'I'm in space, I'm floating around.'

Mum wasn't sure whether to believe either Suzy or Connie. It was not unusual for them to make things up and they also knew a lot of secret places to hide.

'Let's wait a couple of hours,' said Dad 'They'll get hungry and want some food soon.'

'Not with hundreds of cheese sandwiches they won't.'

Dad realised his mistake.

'Well they'll need to go to the toilet soon,' he said.

'I meant to mention that to you,' said Mum. 'The bathroom's gone.'

'Gone?' said Dad.

'Yes look,' said Mum. They walked over to the bathroom, there were just bare walls there. The toilet, sink and bath had all disappeared.

Dad suddenly looked very worried. 'I think they really must be in space,' he said his voice trembling.

# Chapter 13

# The journey part two

Meanwhile the girls were having a whale of a time. Suzy was practising all her gymnastic moves while occasionally reaching out to catch a soft toy as it floated past. Connie was eating the cheese sandwiches while sat in the sleeping bag and looking at one of her books using a torch.

They had had some more conversations with Mum and Dad but now the sound was too faint for them to hear each other.

It had been very dark and they didn't know whether it was day or night. The moon was getting brighter and brighter and almost filling the view from the windows. They were getting nearer and nearer.

'If we go to bed now we will have arrived at the moon when we wake up,' said Suzy. 'But we must brush our teeth first.' Connie followed Suzy into the bathroom.

They found their toothbrushes and toothpaste sellotaped to the wall and brushed up and down. After that they let go and the brushes went flying off into the other part of the rocket.

They floated off to their sleeping bags. Suzy remembering to grab a book and three soft toys as they flew past her. She picked up her walkie-talkie pressed the button and said 'Suzy to Mum over,' but there was only a crackly noise. 'We're too far away,' she said to Connie. But Connie had already fallen asleep.

Suzy lay awake for a while thinking about tomorrow. What would the moon look like? Would the space suits work? How many soft toys would she take with her? She had a look at the guide, there were a few pictures of the moon from space but no pictures of what it would look like when you were actually there. Well they would find out tomorrow. She shut the book and fell asleep immediately.

## Chapter 14

# On the moon

It was morning, or was it, the girls had no idea what time it was but it was quite bright inside the rocket. Everything had stopped flying around and when the girls got out of the sleeping bags it was as if there was a heavy weight attached to each of their legs.

Suzy said, matter-of-factly, 'We must be on the moon.' She dragged her legs over to the windows and pulled back the curtains. 'Wow, come and have a look Connie, we're on the moon.' Connie struggled over to the window.

'On the moon. On the moon, On the moon,' she sang.

'Let's go out,' said Connie.

'No, wait,' said Suzy. 'I have to remember what we have to do. I know, we have to put on our space suits.' Connie wanted to go out straightaway but Suzy made sure she put on all of the parts of the space suit. 'We have to take some things with us,' said Suzy.

'Let me think, the balloons and pins. Can you carry three Connie?' Connie could just about manage. Suzy also took three and a pin. 'I might need the guide as well,' said Suzy. But not for the first time it had disappeared and the girls were too impatient to have a good look for it.

'Let's go,' said Connie. They walked over to the door taking care not to knock their saucepans off as they went through. Then they stepped out and burst their balloons.

It was quite cold and they could have done with a coat over their dresses. Their wellingtons sank into the grey dust. The sky was black and they could see hundreds of stars twinkling brightly.

'Look over there,' said Connie pointing up into the sky at a blue circle.

'That must be the earth,' said Suzy. 'Look how faraway it is.'

They were so busy looking at the sky they hadn't looked at the ground. When they did they had a shock. In the distance they could see two girls and further away two more. In fact everywhere they looked in the distance there were two stood together near their rockets. Maybe hundreds of pairs. They all looked about the same age as Suzy and Connie.

They wore space suits but they couldn't see any of them with saucepans on their heads. Suzy walked over to the nearest pair, Connie following.

'Hello my name's Suzy, and this is Connie,' she said.

'I'm Gwen and this is my little sister Rachel,' Gwen said. 'Where are you from?'

'Nottingham,' said Suzy and then added 'On Earth.'

'We're from London,' said Gwen. 'On Earth as well.'

Gwen and Rachel had spacesuits like Suzy had seen in Star Wars and a small oxygen cylinder on their backs. 'Your space suits are a bit unusual,' Gwen said.

'Dad made them,' said Connie proudly, 'and they are very good.'

Suzy didn't say anything but she was beginning to think that Dad could have spent more time making the space suits and the rocket.

Connie was looking at the soft monkey that Rachel was carrying and wishing that she had bought her own.

'Do you want to see our rocket?' said Gwen.

'Yes please,' said Suzy. They walked into a gleaming silver rocket inside there were two comfy beds, a metal cupboard with all sorts of food, yoghurts, chocolates, fruit juice, fruit, vitamin tablets. Suzy and Connie helped themselves to the chocolate bars. They knew they would have to go back to their rocket and cheese sandwiches soon.

Gwen was holding the *Young Girls' Guide to going to the Moon*. It looked exactly the same as Suzy's.

'Does your book keep disappearing?' asked Suzy.

'Yes,' said Gwen. 'I think when I want to read it, it appears, then when another girl wants to read it, it disappears and they can read it.'

Just then the book disappeared and they could see one of the girls in the distance reading it.

'We can't stay long,' said Suzy. 'We haven't any more balloons to burst.' Gwen and Rachel looked at her with a puzzled look on their faces.

The girls hugged each other and then Suzy and Connie left to return to their rocket.

They walked through their door shutting it behind them.

'What do we do now?' asked Connie.

'I've forgotten,' replied Suzy. ' I need to look at the guide.' The guide was now back in front of her on the floor. Suzy turned to the chapter *How to get Home*.

The book said

1. Make sure all your doors and windows are shut

So Suzy and Connie did that.

2. Get into your sleeping bags. They did that.

3. Press the remote control to start the engine.

Suzy couldn't reach the lawnmower from the sleeping bag. So she had to move it closer to the sleeping bag and get back in.

'Do I have to keep the saucepan on?' said Connie.

'I think so,' said Suzy. 'The book doesn't say anything about saucepans.'

Suzy pressed the switch on the lawn mower to start the engine but nothing happened. She pressed it again still nothing. 'Oh no! What shall we do now?'

# Chapter 15

# Take off

Suzy tried the lawnmower switch a few more times, but it was no good.

'Look in the guide,' Connie said. Suzy looked through the guide and noticed the chapter that Dad had decided not to read, *What to do when things go wrong.* In the list of contents there was the heading *What to do when the engine won't start* page 235. Suzy flipped the pages as quickly as she could. Then read the chapter aloud.

'If your engine won't start then your dad will probably have put a spare one in your rocket, try that one.' Suzy was absolutely sure that there was only one lawnmower on board. She read out the next sentence. 'If your dad hasn't left a spare engine then you have to make one from the materials inside your rocket.'

Suzy couldn't think of anything they had that would be any use she had never seen an engine made of balloons, cheese sandwiches or soft toys, She could feel the tears welling up. In desperation she turned to Connie who was singing 'Twinkle, twinkle little star.'

'Listen,' she said. 'How can we make an engine ?' She waited patiently while Connie screwed her eyes up and thought as hard as she had ever done in her life then replied...

'I don't know.'

Suzy slapped her forehead with her hand. It was no good asking Connie she would have to solve the problem herself. Then she had the best idea ever, maybe the lawnmower batteries had stopped working. Fortunately, accidentally, Dad had left some screwdrivers inside the rocket, she picked one up and unscrewed the battery holder on the lawnmower. The batteries had black gunge round the end so she took them out.

She then used the screwdriver to get the batteries out of her walkie-talkie and put them in the lawnmower, then she screwed the holder shut as tightly as possible.

She went back inside the sleeping bag and pressed the switch. The engine spluttered into life and the rocket lifted off the surface. The girls waited until the moon was looking smaller through the windows. They got out of their sleeping bags, once again they were floating.

'I've done it,' cried Suzy. 'We're on our way back home.'

# Chapter 16

## The chocolate days

The rocket sped on its way towards Earth, the blue globe becoming bigger and bigger in the windows. Inside Suzy and Connie had perfected some more gymnastic moves especially somersaults which could take them from one side of the rocket to the other. Instead of eating some by now stale cheese sandwiches they had been eating the chocolate bars they had taken from Gwen's rocket.

The chocolate wrappers now added to the objects that were flying around, balloons, crusts and bits of cheese, soft toys, toothbrushes and books. They occasionally had a nap in their sleeping bags, and the time passed by.

'Will we be home soon?' asked Connie. 'I want to see Mum and Dad.'

'Not long now,' said Suzy. Just then they heard a crackling noise.

'Walkie-talkie,' Connie said.

'Where is it?' said Suzy.

'I can't see it,' said Connie.

After a few minutes of floating around Suzy finally saw it and reached out her hand to grab it as it raced past.

Excitedly she pressed the button 'Suzy to Mummy or Daddy over' Mum's voice came over very faintly.

'Where are you over?'

'We're still on the rocket but we will be home soon over.'

'We've missed you so much over.'

Connie grabbed the walkie-talkie from Suzy. 'We've eaten lots of chocolate,' she said.

The walkie-talkie stopped working. The Earth was so big they could only see a bit of it through the window. They suddenly stopped floating and it felt as if a giant panda was pinning them down on to their sleeping bags. A few balloons popped.

The girls were feeling frightened. They glanced out of the window and could see green fields, trees and houses, then they could see the river going through Nottingham and then their house. There was a loud bang, the rocket had stopped moving.

'I think we're home,' said Suzy. She tried to get to the door but her legs wouldn't move. Just then the door opened and it was Mum and Dad with tears streaming down their faces. They reached over and pulled the girls out of the rocket onto the cotton wool floor.

'We missed you so much,' said Mum. They all hugged each other.

'I did lots of gambols,' said Connie.

# Chapter 17

# Back home

In the days that followed Mum and Dad tried to get back to normal. Mum wrote a letter to the school to explain why Suzy would not be there for the next week. It read, Dear Miss Litherland, Suzy will not be coming to school this week because she has chickenpox. Suzy had to have red spots painted on her in case anyone from school saw her.

The girls couldn't stop telling Mum and Dad about their trip. 'Look at my somersaults and floating,' said Connie who not for the first time jumped up and crashed to the floor adding to a growing number of bruises.

Suzy said 'There were lots of other girls on the moon. We talked to Gwen and Rachel. They live in London. Can we go and see them?'

'Do you know their surname or address?' asked Mum.

Suzy shook her head. 'We won't be able to find them,' said Mum. 'Millions of people live in London.'

Suzy didn't give up that easily. 'Can we go to the moon again and see them there?'

Mum inwardly groaned 'I'll think about it later,' she said hoping that Suzy would forget about it.

Mum and Dad had been busy fitting a new living room carpet. They were very pleased to have their bathroom back. Suzy and Connie's bedroom was painted black with white paper stars and the moon stuck on the walls.

Suzy and Connie asked for stories about the moon every night. *Young Girls' Guide to Going to the Moon* had disappeared while they were flying back and hadn't reappeared since so the girls went to the library to get some other books.

'Hello again,' said Dad to the librarian, but she did not appear to recognise him. There were no books just about the moon but there was a colourful book about the Solar System which Dad took out. This became Suzy's favourite book. Connie listened every night when Suzy read about all the other planets.

A few weeks later the book had to be returned to the library. Dad went along with Suzy who reluctantly handed it over. On the way out of the library Suzy said, 'I want to go to Mars.'

# Punch and Judy

# Chapter 1

# The conversation

It was Friday evening. Suzy and Connie had just finished performing their latest Punch and Judy show. Mr Punch and Judy were sitting in their toy box alongside the other puppets who had been in the show, Baby, Crocodile and Joey.

Mr Punch was putting a bandage on Judy's arm covering up a bruise from the normal bashing she had received as part of the show, Baby was massaging Mr Punch's neck where the crocodile had bitten him and Joey who had escaped without any injuries this time was rubbing the crocodile's nose where he had been hit by Mr Punch's stick.

Once all the knocks had been dealt with Mrs Punch (Judy) put on the kettle and they all had a cup of tea and some biscuits while discussing that afternoon's show.

' It was particularly bad this afternoon,' said Judy.

'Why can't we have a show without getting hurt?'

'You always say that,' said Mr Punch. 'But you know the children like the show as it is, and we can't stop them making us hit each other.'

'It's not us hitting each other,' said Baby. 'It's you hitting all of us.'

'I think we should speak to our cousins again,' said Joey. 'They seem to have been successful with a gentler type of show.'

'Yes but they don't have Suzy and Connie doing the shows,' said Mr Punch.

'Still I think we should try again,' said Crocodile.

The puppets agreed they would speak to their cousins tomorrow morning to see what could be done.

# Chapter 2

# The phone call

Next morning, once the house was empty, Mr Punch made a call to his cousins.

'Hello!' said his cousin Mark.

'Hello, it's Mr Punch here, how is everyone?'

'We're fine,' Mark replied.

'We're having some problems with our show,' Mr Punch explained. 'We wanted to talk about your show.'

'OK,' said his cousin, 'What do you want to know?'

'You decided to have a gentler show,' said Punch.

'Yes,' said Mark, 'To begin with we just changed my stick to a stick of celery.'

'Did that work?' said Punch.

'It did for us, no one got hurt but the children didn't like it, so we had to make more changes.'

'How?' asked Punch

'First of all we changed some names. I changed from

Mr Punch to Mr Pat, and Judy became Julie, so we became the Pat and Julie show. Baby and Joey kept their names.'

'And what about Crocodile?' Mr Punch interrupted.

'Well we couldn't do a gentler show with a crocodile in it so we had to let him go.'

'What else did you do?'

'Joey wrote a new story for the show,' said Mark.

'We then stuck it on the fridge for our children to find. They put on some shows for their parents and other children. I must admit, not all the audience liked it and Joey is thinking of making some more changes. We could come over with our children and let you see it if you like.'

'I think we would like that. Can you come over on Sunday morning?'

'Yes,' said Mark 'We'll do that.'

'Great,' said Punch. 'By the way what happened to Crocodile?'

' Oh he's fine he goes around the county talking about all the shows he has done and answering questions from the audience. He's more successful than ever.'

'We'll see you tomorrow then, we'll look forward to our first Pat and Julie show.'

Punch put the phone down. He wondered if a gentler show would be popular and could he get used to being called Mr Pat.

## Chapter 3

# The visit

It was 10 o'clock on Sunday morning. Suzy and Connie were watching TV while their parents, David and Vicky were clearing up from breakfast. Suddenly they were interrupted by the sound of the doorbell.

David opened the front door and had a big surprise. Rachel and Tom were there with their children Bobby and Gwen, Suzy and Connie's cousins. Between them they were carrying a large plastic box.

'Hi, are you ready for our Pat and Julie show?' said Tom. David had no idea what Tom was talking about and they weren't at all ready.

'I didn't know you were coming today,' he said. 'Did you Vicky?' Vicky shook her head.

'But we got a text from you inviting us,' said Rachel.

' Well we didn't send it,' said David 'And I don't think Suzy would have been able to send one, so it's a bit of a mystery, but come on in.'

'So where shall we do our Pat and Julie show' asked Tom.

'What's a Pat and Julie show?' asked David.

'It's a bit like Punch and Judy without any hitting. The children said the puppets told them about it, of course we didn't believe that, but we pretended we did.'

'We'll get our stage out,' said Vicky. 'Look your cousins are here.'

Suzy and Connie looked up briefly from the Peppa Pig episode they were watching and then looked back at it.

'They're going to do a Pat and Julie show, it's a bit like Punch and Judy'

Once the words Punch and Judy had been spoken that changed everything. Suzy turned the TV off and Connie got their puppets out to sit beside her on the sofa.

Bobby and Gwen got their puppets out of the plastic box and went round the back of the stage. Bobby shouted 'The show is about to begin,' and then they started going through the story that Joey had written.

Mr Pat (Bobby): It's such a nice day today let's take Baby to the park.

Julie (Gwen) That's a good idea I'll go and get her.

Baby (Gwen) I've had a long sleep . I want to go to the park now.

Mr Pat, Julie and Bobby walk across the stage singing Let's go to the park, Let's go to the park.

Joey (Bobby) They've now reached the park

Baby (Gwen) Can I go on the swing?

Mr Pat (Bobby) Of course you can my dear

Joey (Bobby) Holds a wooden swing and sits Baby on it

Julie (Gwen) Oh he's really enjoying it!

Joey (Bobby) The end.

It had suddenly gone very quiet. 'Did you enjoy that , Suzy?' asked David. There was a long pause then Suzy replied.

'It was quite good,' though secretly she thought it was really boring.

'And what about you Connie?' Vicky asked.

'No it was rubbish.'

David and Vicky tried to smile but Bobby and Gwen were near to crying.

'Thanks for the show,' said Vicky. 'It was lovely. We

have to do our shopping now, we'll give you a call to arrange to meet you soon.' Bobby and Gwen collected their puppets and waved goodbye. They all hugged on the way out.

'That was weird,' said Vicky. ' How could they have got a text inviting them? You didn't really like the show , did you Suzy?'

'No , it wasn't exciting at all, the crocodile wasn't even in it and no one got hurt.'

'Well that's a good thing,' said David.

'No it's more fun when Mr Punch hits the others with his stick, that's the bit I like best.'

# Chapter 4

# The meeting

Mr Punch, Judy, Baby, Joey and Crocodile had a meeting about the show they had seen.

'I liked it,' said Judy. 'Julie and Baby were so happy.'

'That's true,' said Mr Punch. 'But Suzy and Connie were very bored couldn't we have just a bit of hitting in it to make it more interesting.'

'No that's not the way to do it,' said Joey. 'I need to keep the gentler parts of their story but add something to it.'

'Yes like hitting,' said Mr Punch.

'Shut up,' shouted all the others.

'I've got an idea,' said Joey. 'Why don't we all write our own Punch and Judy story and then we can decide which one we think is the best.'

'Brilliant!' said Mr Punch. 'I'm sure you're all going to like mine.'

'We'll see about that,' said Judy.

'I've got a good idea already,' said Baby.

'Let's wait till next week then we'll go through all the stories,' said Joey.

They all nodded , except Crocodile who was wondering if he needed to look for another job, he couldn't imagine that anyone would like a more gentle type of crocodile.

Next week they all met in the living room when the house was empty.

'I'll go first,' said Mr Punch. ' It was a stormy dark night in autumn and …..'

'Can you cut out the introduction and get straight to the point,' said Joey.

Mr Punch looked a bit upset but continued 'It's Baby's birthday.  Me and Judy make a birthday cake but Judy falls into the cake mixture and when I take her out I accidentally put her onto the knife I was using to smooth out the icing and I cut her leg off. Me and Baby go and visit her in hospital where the doctor (Joey) sews the leg back on and they all live happily ever after.

'That doesn't sound too gentle to me,' said Judy. 'I'm not sure I'll like having my leg cut off.'

'Well let's wait till we've heard the others,' said Joey.

Next it was Judy's turn 'Baby decides he would like to buy a pet. They all go to the pet shop, Baby tries playing with the rabbits, the guinea pigs and hamsters but decides he wants something bigger, a lion in fact. The pet shop says they don't sell lions so they buy a rabbit instead. Baby gets to know his new rabbit and to love it and everyone lives happily ever after.'

'I'll go now,' said Baby. 'It's Baby's first day at school and he is a bit worried that he won't make any friends. He doesn't want to follow his dad's advice (Mr Punch) to hit everyone with a stick who doesn't want to play with him, instead he cooks some biscuits with his mum Judy and shares them with all the other children in his class. Because of this he becomes very popular and everyone lives happily ever after.'

'Crocodile?' asked Joey.

'I haven't written anything,' said Crocodile. 'I don't want to do a Punch and Judy show unless I can bite people, and I don't think you want me to do that anymore.'

'Quite right!' said Judy.

'What about you Joey?' asked Mrs Punch.

'Well my plan was to listen to your stories then make a new one mixing up all the ideas you'd had.

'That's not fair,' said Mr Punch. 'We've all been working so hard and you've just been sitting back and waiting.'

'Well he'll have to do some work now,' said Judy. 'And we know he's the cleverest so I think we should let him do that, put your hands up if you agree.'

Judy and Baby agreed, Crocodile couldn't decide and Mr Punch disagreed.

'I agree of course,' said Joey. So it was three agreeing one against and one undecided.

'All right then,' said Joey. 'I'll work on a new story for next week.'

# Chapter 5

# Joey's story

The puppets had gathered together again, waiting breathlessly for Joey's story.

'Is there any hitting in it?' asked Punch.

'Of course not,' replied Joey.

'Do I get a leg cut off?' asked Judy.

'No, I removed that bit,' said Joey.

'Am I in it?' asked Crocodile.

'Will you just be quiet and let me start,' said Joey trying hard to keep his temper. He waited till they were all silent then he began.

'It's Baby's birthday tomorrow but Punch and Judy can't decide what present to get him. When they ask him he says he wants a pet lion. They look in the Punch and Judy weekly magazine, but there are no lions wanting to join a show. There are a few snakes looking for work but neither of them want a slippery snake in their group.

They ask Joey to find a lion but it has to be a little one. Mr Punch doesn't want it to become the leader, that's his position he thinks.

The next day it is Baby's birthday his sixth, quite old for a baby, but Baby will always be Baby. When he wakes up he looks all around for a lion puppet but can't find one.

Judy says "Let's make some birthday biscuits for your school friends."

They mix flour and eggs together and for a few minutes Baby forgets all about his present. Judy and Baby make thirty biscuits, two for each of Baby's friends. They place them on some kitchen paper to cool down. Before putting them in a box they count them and discover that five have gone.

"Something's wrong," says Judy "you count them Mr Punch."

Mr Punch counts them carefully but there are only ten left now. Neither Mr Punch, Judy nor Baby had noticed a lion roaming about the kitchen who had carried off most of the biscuits in its mouth.

Just then Baby spots the lion coming back to finish off the rest of the biscuits.

"My present's come," he cries. "Come here little lion".
Even though the lion is twice Baby's size.

The lion strolls over and Baby strokes it. Baby and the
lion make some more biscuits to take to school. Baby
has a lovely time at school telling his friends how he had
baked them with his new pet lion.

'Well what do you think?' asked Joey.

'It was all right, 'said Judy. 'But I would have liked
the lion to be locked up in jail for stealing the biscuits.
I thought it was good that no one knew what had
happened to the biscuits only the children watching
would know.'

'I loved it,' said Baby. 'Especially that we can eat all
the biscuits after the show.' Even Crocodile seemed to be
smiling but you never could tell with him.

'I'll write it down,' said Joey. 'So Suzy and Connie can
perform it in front of their mum, dad and cousins. If they
like it then we can perform the show all over the world.'

'Just one question,' said Punch. 'How are we going to
get a lion to join us?'

'No problem,' said Joey with a funny expression on his
face. 'Just leave it with me.'

# Chapter 6

# Success

The next day Suzy found the script for the new Punch and Judy show stuck on the fridge with a magnet. Suzy and Connie discussed what to do next.

'We should practise, and then we can invite our cousins to come and see it,' said Suzy.

Connie thought. 'Can we tell Mum and Dad about it?' she asked.

'I think we should keep it secret for the moment, until we have finished our practice.' advised Suzy.

They decided that Suzy would show the Mr Punch and Joey puppets while Connie would have Baby and Judy. They both wanted to be the lion but in the end they decided they would share.

A few things went wrong in their rehearsals in the first one Baby accidentally fell into the biscuit mixture and then in the next one they couldn't find the Punch and

Judy magazine. They found it in the kitchen bin covered in bits of broccoli so they had to use one of Connie's *In the Night Garden* magazines instead. They hoped no one would notice the change. They still hadn't found a lion puppet so they practised with Connie's toy monkey.

After three rehearsals Suzy said 'I think we're ready, we ought to ask Mum to invite our cousins now. You do it Connie, you're better at getting your own way.' So Connie put on a very sad face and went to ask Mum. At first Mum said no they were too busy at the moment. But then Connie put on her even sadder face which involved making her bottom lip tremble and Mum had to give in. The cousins were to come on Sunday.

Come Sunday and Uncle Tom, Aunty Rachel, Bobby and Gwen were sat in the living room eagerly awaiting the show. Their puppets were also there and of course Mum and Dad.

Before the show started Suzy stood in front of the stage to make an announcement. 'Ladies and Gentlemen Boys and Girls here is our show called *Punch and Judy – The New Generation,* written by Suzy and Connie. (Suzy didn't know who had written it and was sure no one would find out that it wasn't the girls).

The audience clapped while Suzy and Connie gave a deep bow then disappeared behind the stage. To their surprise there was a puppet lion there. Crocodile was missing but as he wasn't in the new show nobody was bothered.

Suzy and Connie performed the show just as they had practised. The audience shouted when the lion was stealing the biscuits and there were lots of ah's when Baby stroked the lion at the end. Everyone felt happy with the story.

After the performance the puppets sat in their box discussing the show while crunching on the biscuits. 'Suzy and Connie did it very well,' said Mr Punch.

'And the parents and other children really enjoyed it,' said Judy.

' I'm very pleased,' chipped in Joey. It's so difficult to write a completely new show that everyone likes.'

'I like these biscuits,' said Baby.

'What did you think, Crocodile?' asked Joey.

Crocodile cleared the biscuit crumbs from his jaw. ' I don't think anyone noticed it was me inside the lion fur.

I had a bigger part than normal and it kept me in your show so I'm delighted.'

Suzy and Connie continued to present their new show at their friends' birthday parties with great success. Every so often a message on the fridge asked them to do the old show with Judy insisting that they use a stick of celery instead of Mr Punch's stick.

# Unicorn Tale

# Chapter 1

## A plan

Suzy and Connie were bored, bored, bored. It was Thursday afternoon. Mum was at work, Dad was working at home and they had just watched four episodes of Peppa Pig, four episodes they had seen at least ten times before.

'Let's see what Dad's doing,' said Connie. Dad was at the table looking at the computer screen. There was paper all around and Suzy could sense that he wasn't too happy.

'What are you doing?' she asked.

'Oh it's just some report I have to do for work.'

'A report of what?' she continued. Dad thought it was probably best to try and explain so that the girls would run out of questions and go back to watching the television.

'Mr Brown wants me to report on sales prospects

for our new adhesive product.' he said. 'So I'm doing a spreadsheet of estimated sales in different businesses.' he added.

Suzy looked blank and Connie just stood by him with her mouth open in an expression she often adopted when she didn't have a clue what someone had just said to her. Suzy tried a question.

'Can we help?'

'I don't think you're too good at spreadsheets,' Dad replied.

'Is that like when we make our bed?' Suzy said.

'No that's bedsheets,' said Dad who had now realised he had taken the wrong approach in trying to explain his work.

'I'm trying to make some money by selling glue' he said.

At last Connie had a flicker of understanding.

'So it's like someone buying our Pritt stick?' she said.

'A bit,' said Dad.

'Can we sell our Pritt stick then?' said Suzy.

' I don't think we have any,' said Dad. 'But I'll tell you what. Why don't you play a game of shops where you sell different things to customers?'

'I can be the shopkeeper,' said Connie, 'and you can be the customer.'

' No, Suzy can be the customer while I get on with my work,' he said.

'That's a good idea,' said Suzy.

They moved away from Dad and Connie put a lot of toys on top of her toy box. Suzy pretending to come into the shop to buy something.

They happily played at this game for half an hour during which time Connie had sold all her toys to Suzy. 'Can I have my toys back now?' Connie asked.

'No,' said Suzy 'They're mine now, I paid for them.'

'But you didn't give me anything, only pretend money.' Suzy thought about this a bit and realised it wasn't completely fair.

'You can have them back,' she said. 'But this has given me an idea. You know the toy shop in the village?'

'Yes.'

'Well they have a toy monkey that you wanted and a toy unicorn that I wanted.'

'I know,' said Connie. ' But Mummy said we had spent all our money from Christmas so we would have to wait.'

'Yes,' said Suzy. ' But what if we could earn our own money.'

'How?' asked Connie.

'I've got a plan that just might work,' said Suzy mysteriously.

Chapter 2

# Getting the money

Next morning Suzy and Connie woke up early. Connie had remembered what Suzy had said yesterday. 'So how can we get the money to buy the toy animals,' she said.

'I've already got some money,' said Suzy. 'I've got two pounds from the tooth fairy and we need eight pounds for the toys.'

'So how much more do we need?' asked Connie.

' That's eight take way two,' said Suzy who had just started take aways. 'So that's urr , urr . I don't remember, let's ask Dad.' They went into Mum and Dad's bedroom. Dad was fast asleep, snoring. 'What's eight take away two?' they shouted together.

'That will be six,' muttered Dad and then fell back to sleep immediately.

The girls went downstairs. Suzy sat down on the sofa and started to think. 'That means I have to lose six teeth,' she said. 'That could take ages.'

'I could lose some as well,' said Connie.

'No you're too young you haven't got any loose ones yet, but I've got two that are a bit loose maybe you could help me get them out. I know how to do it.'

Suzy got some string from the kitchen and cut off a length. 'Now I'll go the top stair, you tie the string round one of my loose teeth then hold the string and jump down three stairs.'

Connie tried to do what Suzy had said. She tied the string to Suzy's loose tooth and jumped down three stairs, but the knot came loose so the tooth didn't come out.

'Let's try again,' said Suzy. 'But this time I'll tie the knot round the tooth.' Suzy did that then Connie jumped down again, the string pulled on Suzy's tooth, but instead of the tooth coming out Suzy tumbled forward bumped into Connie and they both fell to the bottom of the stairs Connie landing first and Suzy landed on top of her. Connie started crying.

Mum came to see what had happened. 'What on earth is going on?' she said. Connie kept on crying but Suzy looked quite happy.

' We slipped and fell down the stairs. And Connie knocked two of her teeth out, perhaps the tooth fairy will come tonight.'

Sure enough when Connie woke up the next morning there were two pound coins on her bedside table. She leapt onto Suzy's bed in excitement.

'Look the tooth fairy's been, I've got two pounds.' Suzy smiled.

'You've knocked my two loose teeth out as well,' she said. 'If we wait till tomorrow morning the tooth fairy will have left two more pounds and we can go to the toy shop.' (Suzy hadn't realised they would only have six pounds instead of the eight they needed).

'Why can't the tooth fairy come in the morning?' asked Connie.

'Mum said we weren't allowed to ever see her, so she always comes when everyone is asleep.'

'Why can't we see her?' demanded Connie.

'Because, er, I don't know,' answered Suzy. 'But that's what Mum said.'

The girls found it hard to get through the next day

without thinking about going to the toy shop. They asked Dad over and over again if they could go there when he went to the supermarket. Dad kept answering that they would go as long as he could finish his work in time.

Before they went to bed Suzy and Connie had both cleared a space for their new toys. 'I'll call the unicorn 'Horsey,' said Suzy. 'I'll call my monkey Horsey,' said Connie.

'You can't do that, we'll get mixed up,' said Suzy. But Connie had fallen asleep so she didn't hear.

# Chapter 3

# The toy shop

It was Saturday but Mum still had to go to work, Dad had finished working at home and was looking forward to going out with the girls. Suzy was jumping about holding the two pound coins that had appeared on her bedside cabinet. She had tried to stay awake as long as possible in the hope that she would catch a glimpse of the tooth fairy, but in the end she had nodded off.

The girls finished their breakfast, put their hats and coats on and were ready to go out. 'It's only half past seven,' said Dad. 'You're going to have to wait till the shops open.'

'Aw,' said Connie.

'Can we queue outside the toy shop,' said Suzy.

'No it's far too early,' said Dad. 'You go and play in the living room and I'll clear up, the time will go by before you know it.' Suzy and Connie went into the other room

and started playing shops again but they soon g〔 .
of that. Then they went back into the kitchen.

'Can we go now?' It was still early but Dad thought
they could leave, it wouldn't be too long a wait if the
shop was shut.

'Have you got your money?' he asked . They had
both forgotten. They quickly ran upstairs to pick up the
pound coins, two pounds for Connie, 4 pounds for Suzy,
then ran downstairs as quickly as possible and stood by
the front door.

'Right, let's go flo,' said Dad. The girls skipped
down the street towards the village. 'You know the way
Connie, you go first'. This was a cunning ploy on Dad's
part because although Connie thought she knew the
way, she didn't, so it would slow down the trip to the
shop and they would have less time to queue.

Eventually the toy shop came into view. 'Look, there's
the unicorn,' shouted Suzy.

'And my monkey,' added Connie.

Dad had a close look, 'They're four pounds each that's
eight pounds you've only got six. We're going to have to
come back another time.'

…e and Connie lied down on the

…, to move. Dad would have liked to be

…one else what to do, but he was on his

…ways complained if he interrupted her at

work.

After five minutes the girls were about to give up when Dad said calmly 'Let's go into the shop and see what we can do.' Suzy and Connie immediately changed their glum expressions into those of happiness as they pushed the door open and entered the shop.

'I'll speak,' said Dad.

But instead Connie said to the lady in the shop 'We want the unicorn and monkey but we haven't got enough money.'

'How much *have* you got?' said the lady.

'Six pounds,' said Suzy.

'There is something I could do,' said the lady mysteriously. 'Just follow me'. They all followed her behind the counter through a door into a small garden. In the far corner was what looked like a small white pony, but as they got nearer it turned towards them and they could clearly see a small horn on its forehead. Suzy was the first to react.

'Wow, it's a unicorn.'

'A unicorn,' echoed Connie.

'A unicorn,' echoed Dad. 'It's not real,' said Dad recovering himself slightly.

' Go ahead and pat it,' the lady said. They all approached it cautiously.

Connie went right up to its nose and patted it 'It is real Daddy,' she cried.

'Do you want to look after it for two weeks?' asked the lady. 'Just give me your money and you can take it away tonight. It has to be dark so it can be a secret otherwise the police will want to take it away to a zoo.'

Dad really should have thought this through but he was still shocked what's more he could feel the girls staring at him waiting for him to say yes. 'Yes,' he said handing over the money I'll be back for it this evening will eight o'clock be all right?' The lady nodded. They followed her back into the shop.

'I'll see you tonight then,' said the lady. 'Don't forget to keep it a secret.'

On the way back home the girls couldn't stop talking

about it. They had already decided to call it Horsey.
As they approached home Dad said 'Remember you
mustn't tell your friends about it and especially don't tell
Mummy, you know she can't keep a secret.'

## Chapter 4

# Horsey comes home

'I'm just going to the running club,' shouted Mum from the kitchen.

'When will you be back?' asked Dad.

'About half past eight.'

That gave Dad about an hour to go to the shop, walk Horsey back, settle her in, and start getting the girls ready for bed.

As soon as Mum had left he dashed to the door put the girls' bikes out and off they went. Suzy led the way this time, Connie following and Dad running trying to keep up with them.

They reached the shop and the lady greeted them.

'I've just fed her,' she said. 'I hope you've got plenty of food for her.'

'I hadn't thought of that,' said Dad.

'And she'll need some bedding.'

'Will she?' said Dad with a worried look. 'I hadn't thought of that either.'

'You have got somewhere for her to stay I suppose,' asked the lady.

'Of course,' said Dad.

'Where Daddy?' asked Suzy.

'Er I'll tell you when we get back,' Dad replied.

The lady led them into the garden. It had already turned dark but in the far corner they could see the unicorn wearing a sort of coat covering its head and body, only its eyes and ears were peeping out.

'Now remember it must be a secret,' said the lady. 'Don't talk to anybody in the street, I'll see you in two weeks at the same time.' She opened the back gate and Dad lead Horsey by its reins into the street.

'Goodbye' they whispered. Just before they set off Suzy asked

'Have you got some straw we could take for the bedding?'

'I've got a bit,' said the lady and returned with a bag which Suzy hung over her handlebars.

They started off home. It was quiet in the village but

they were all frightened they would be discovered and Horsey taken to the zoo. They were lucky and reached home without seeing anyone. 'Where are we going to put her?' asked Suzy.

'Let me think,' said Dad.

'I know,' said Connie. 'We can put her in the loft.'

'Good idea,' said Dad. 'But I don't think we'll be able to get her up the loft ladder.'

'Well what about the garage?'

'Mum would be suspicious if I moved the car out to make room.'

'I know,' said Suzy. 'She can go in the shed at the bottom of the garden, no one ever goes there.'

'That will work,' said Dad .They led Horsey into the back garden took off her coat and went to open the shed door. 'Oh no it's locked!' he exclaimed. 'You hold the reins,' he said to Suzy. 'I'll see if I can find the key.' He dashed into the house grabbed a bunch of keys by the front door and returned to the shed. The first three keys didn't fit but then the next one much to his relief turned and the door was open. The shed was full of rubbish, old paint pots, spare bike wheels, tools that no one had used in years and old newspapers.

'We need to take all these out,' said Dad, 'and hide them under Horsey's coat.' Mum would be back soon so they had to rush. Finally the shed was empty, Suzy laid the straw on the floor and they tried to get Horsey to go in, but she wasn't happy and started neighing.

'Shh,' whispered Suzy.

'I'll get some food and water,' said Dad. 'You stay with her I won't be long.' A minute later he returned with a bucket of water and a pan full of porridge oats. 'That will do,' he said. They patted Horsey on her nose and gently led her into the shed, amazingly she went in this time and started to drink from the bucket.

'Quick!' said Dad. 'Get out!' He locked the door.

'Now get ready for bed as quickly as you can before Mum gets back. Don't forget it's a secret.'

The girls ran as fast as they could stopping only to put on their pyjamas they jumped into bed just as the door opened and Mum came in.

'Wow it's quiet,' she said. 'Is everything all right?'

'Yes the girls have just got into bed.'

Mum went upstairs to say goodnight. 'Did you have a

nice time with Dad?' she asked.

'Yes we went to the toy shop,' said Connie and then realised it was supposed to be a secret.

'Oh, you were playing shops again,' said Mum.

'Yes,' said Dad rather quickly. Mum kissed the girls and then Mum and Dad went downstairs.

'That was my most exciting day,' said Connie.

'It will be even better tomorrow,' said Suzy picking a piece of straw from her hair. They laid down listening to see if they could hear any sound from the shed, but it was quiet.

'Good night Horsey,' they said quietly.

# Chapter 5

# Shopping

Normally on Sunday everyone would get up a bit later. But for Dad he couldn't get to sleep at all, things were getting so complicated. He got out of bed at three in the morning and went downstairs to have a think in peace while everyone else was fast asleep.

One thing that was puzzling him was how the lady at the toy shop had managed to get a unicorn in her back garden. Maybe she had stolen it, but from where? Then was her warning correct, would the police really take Horsey to a zoo? There wasn't a zoo near their house. It was a complete mystery.

More importantly where could he keep Horsey for two weeks, there was so little space in the shed, it was a well known fact that unicorns needed plenty of space to sleep in.

If he was going to keep Horsey a secret then he had

to find a way to get her some food and bedding without letting Vicky know. How could he do that in time for Horsey's breakfast when the shops didn't open until everyone was awake on Sunday? Did he even know what time unicorns had breakfast? How could he get enough to last for two weeks? Just what could they do with Horsey for two weeks while keeping her secret?

Now for most people the simplest plan would be to tell Vicky about Horsey, take the unicorn back to the shop tonight and forget all about it. Everyone would think Suzy and Connie were just making up stories if they told anyone about it.

However Dad never gave in. Here was a problem that must be solved, a challenge that must be faced, a stupid mistake that must be put right. Gradually he formed a plan in his mind. Satisfied he lay down on the sofa and was soon fast asleep. He was woken up at nine o'clock by Suzy jumping on top of him.

'Are you all right?' Mum asked.

'Yes I came downstairs to get a drink and I must have fallen asleep.'

'I'll get you a coffee to wake you up we need to go to

the supermarket soon before Connie's gymnastic lesson and then Suzy and Connie are going to Jack's party this afternoon.'

Sometime in this busy day Dad had to find a way to look after Horsey. It would not be easy.

Suzy and Connie came over to him and whispered 'Can we see Horsey now?'

'Let me think,' said Dad.

'Quickly come with me to the shed.' Dad, still in his pyjamas, and the girls, ran over the grass to the shed. Dad hadn't got the keys so he had to lift the girls up so they could look through the small window. Horsey was awake but lying down, she didn't look too well.

They returned to the house just as Mum had come into the living room with a cup of coffee. 'What are you all up to ?' she asked in an amused tone.

'It's a secret,' said Dad. ' I'll tell you about it later'. He hoped that she would forget about it but Mum very rarely forgot things.

He drank his coffee quickly, whenever Mum wasn't watching he looked at the girls and put his finger to his lips to remind the girls to keep quiet about the unicorn.

When he was ready they all set off in their car to the supermarket.

Mum had written out the shopping list. They took a large trolley and stated to buy things from the list. Mum wanted to get a new bucket because the one in the kitchen had mysteriously disappeared. Dad saw his chance.

'Why don't you get one from Wilkinsons?' he said. 'I'll carry on with the rest of the shopping here.'

'OK,' said Mum and off she went.

Dad knew Mum would find other things to buy so he reckoned he had half an hour before she got back.

'Quick,' he said . He left their trolley in the aisle and went to get another one. Then he quickly ran as fast as possible to the breakfast cereal shelves pulling Suzy and Connie behind him.

'What are we doing?' gasped Suzy.

' We need to get Horsey some cereal. I think that's what unicorns eat.'

'Can we get Coco Pops?' asked Connie.

'A very good idea,' said Dad. 'If Mum discovered them we could say it was for you.'

They loaded the packets of Coco Pops into the trolley then they ran over to the pet food section. There was no unicorn straw but there were some packets of rabbit bedding. They loaded up the trolley with those and then went to the checkout.

'Hello Mr Goodwin,' said the sales assistant. 'Have you run out of saucepans yet?'

Dad's strange purchases of saucepans had not been forgotten.

'Ha Ha,' laughed Dad. 'It's just our normal shopping today,' he said as he emptied twenty five packets of Coco Pops and ten bags of rabbit bedding onto the belt. The sales assistant rolled her eyes but said nothing just checking out all the shopping.

Dad paid for it and then had to rush to hide it in the car boot under a blanket. He then ran back into the supermarket picked up the trolley they had left in the aisle and continued buying the things Mum had written on her list.

After five minutes Mum returned with three carrier bags.

'I just bought a few more things,' she said. They

went round the shelves and went to pay for the goods. Unfortunately it was the same assistant as before.

'Hello again,' she said in a friendly manner.

'Hello,' Dad said. After they had paid, Dad said to Mum 'She must have remembered me from last week.'

They loaded all their bags into the boot. Dad frequently looking at the girls with his finger to his lips and Suzy also doing the same thing when Mum wasn't looking.

When they got home they all took the shopping out of the car into the kitchen, but all the supplies for Horsey had to be left under the blanket in the car. Horsey must be getting really hungry by now, thought Dad.

'We need to go to Connie's gym class now,' said Mum. ' Can you get her ready, Suzy, you can help me put this shopping away.' There was just no time to get Horsey's things out of the car.

'If I stay behind, I can wrap the presents up for the party,' suggested Dad.

'Oh all right,' said Mum.

As soon as they had left, Dad went over to the shed. He opened the door took the bucket of water and shut the door as fast as he could so that Horsey couldn't get out. He filled the bucket with fresh water and looked round the kitchen for some food. There was a box of cornflakes they had bought that morning, Dad hoped that would be enough until he found a way to get the Coco Pops out of the car.

He ran back to the shed left the bucket of water and the packet of cornflakes and quickly shut the door. Outside he could hear the sound of Horsey ripping open the cornflakes box. He would have just enough time to iron some clothes for the party that afternoon and lay out the girls' dresses, and wrap their presents. He was feeling exhausted and lay down on the sofa for a few minutes before he heard their car pulling up onto the drive.

# Chapter 6

## Pink daylight

The rest of the day passed by without Dad being able to sneak away to feed Horsey. Later when he had gone to bed he couldn't stop thinking about her. He had decided to set his phone alarm to three o'clock so he could get up to see to Horsey, but he attached his headphones so that he wouldn't wake up anyone else.

Despite all his worries, he fell asleep quickly but woke up after only a short nap. Much to his surprise he was downstairs in the living room, fully dressed. Suzy and Connie were also there. The curtains were open and outside it was daylight but a strange sort of pink light with a rainbow shining brightly in the sky.

'Wait there a minute,' he said. He disappeared outside returning with an armful of Coco Pops boxes and rabbit bedding. 'Follow me.' He opened the French window, they walked over to the shed and Dad opened the door.

Horsey stepped out and started to devour one of the Coco Pops boxes. In the meantime Dad found an old spade and cleared out the bedding replacing it with the rabbit bedding.

Suzy and Connie brushed Horsey's coat. It was the first time they had had a good look at her. 'She's beautiful,' said Suzy. Indeed she was. The light gave her coat a pink glow and she had a thick pink mane which rippled in pink and white colours as she moved. The girls went into the kitchen to replace the bucket with some fresh water, they needed all their strength to carry it out between them. Horsey took a few huge gulps and neighed again.

'Let's take her for a walk,' said Connie.

'OK,' said Dad forgetting they had to keep her secret. They walked out into the street following the path to the park. It was very quiet, there were no cars about.

'Hello Dave,' someone shouted. Dad looked up and saw Jack's dad on the other side of the road. He also had a unicorn with him.

'We're just taking our unicorn to the park,' shouted Suzy.

'Have a good time,' shouted back Jack's dad. Further along they saw other people all accompanied by a unicorn.

When they reached the park Suzy let go of Horsey's reins and off she ran, around the lake, her tail streaming out behind her and neighing at the top of her voice. Suzy and Connie chased after her but couldn't catch up. After a few minutes Horsey came to rest by Dad and the girls, out of breath, joined them.

'Wow that was good,' said Connie.

'Yes maybe we should go back now,' said Suzy.

'No,' said Connie let's get an ice cream.' Dad agreed. He held Horsey's reins and walked over to the ice cream van. There was another unicorn by the van and Horsey made friends with it while Suzy and Connie ate their ice creams.

When they had finished they set off home. There were still more people leading unicorns around the streets. In fact everyone they saw had a unicorn with them. They got home and took Horsey into the garden and then put her back into the shed, Suzy and Connie threw a few boxes of Coco Pops in after her. Horsey looked at them with an unhappy expression. Dad knew it would be a bit uncomfortable in the shed but he couldn't think where else to put her.

'Goodbye Horsey,' they said softly as Dad shut the door.

A tune started playing louder and louder, and Dad woke up he was in bed it was the middle of the night and very dark, his alarm had just gone off.

## Chapter 7

# The dream

The next day was the usual Monday morning rush. Connie had decided she was going to make her own lunch, three boxes of raisins a small packet of crisps and one piece of bread with nothing on it. She crammed these into her lunch box before Mum could check it and replace a pack of raisins with an apple. Suzy had lost her spellings book and wouldn't get dressed until she had found it.

Eventually they were all ready and Mum waved goodbye as she cycled off to her work at the hospital. Dad bundled the girls into the car and set off. There was a lot of traffic on the road so he had to concentrate but he could hear Suzy and Connie talking about the unicorn.

'I had a dream last night,' said Suzy. 'We took Horsey to the park.'

'And I had a chocolate ice cream in my dream,' said Connie.

'That's funny,' said Suzy. 'I had an ice cream too in my dream and so did you, was the sky pink in your dream?'

'Yes it was and there was a rainbow in the sky.'

Dad almost went past the turning into the school. He was shocked. It sounded that the girls had been in the same dream as him. He pulled up outside the school. 'Was I in your dream?' he asked.

'Yes,' replied Suzy, 'You led Horsey to the park and said hello to Jack's dad.'

'Jack's my best friend,' said Connie.

He kissed the girls and watched as they ran off into the school. He wondered, could they all have been in the same dream? Before going into work he drove back home and went through the garden to the shed. He opened the door and there was Horsey with the empty packets of Coco Pops by her, the ones he had left in the dream.

He went to get a fresh bucket of water, replaced the bedding and dropped in some new Coco Pops packets.

Connie's apple was in the kitchen so he left that in the shed as well. Horsey looked a bit happier this morning although she still looked a bit upset when Dad had to close the door and lock her in. I must find somewhere else to keep her, he thought. Maybe there's a stable nearby.

Later that day Dad collected the girls from school. They went into the kitchen and Dad started to cook some fish fingers and beans. The girls were not interested in eating, they wanted to see Horsey. 'You can take her for a walk round the garden, but she needs to go back in the shed before Mum gets back.'

They led Horsey round the garden for a while then Dad pulled the reins off them and put the unicorn back in the shed.

'I want to play with her a bit more,' complained Connie. Just this once Dad could not give in to what Connie wanted.

'She must be hidden before Mum comes back,' he said. 'And you must eat some dinner.' Connie pretended to cry but Dad ignored her.

They went to back into the house. Suzy ate her dinner

but Connie pushed her beans round the plate and just had a small bite from a fish finger.

When Mum came in Connie went up to her and said 'Daddy won't let me play with Horsey.'

Dad quickly grabbed her and whispered 'You must be quiet else the police will take her away.'

'Who's Horsey?' asked Mum.

'Err she's the toy unicorn in the toy shop,' said Dad.

'That's funny you were going to buy her and the monkey on Saturday, what happened?'

'We didn't have enough money,' said Dad trying to keep calm. 'We can go and get them next Saturday.'

Mum thought this was a good sign that Dad was becoming a bit stricter. Normally he would have given in and paid for the toys with his own money.

'Yes, we'll get them next Saturday,' said Suzy backing up Dad's story and pleased to be getting a toy unicorn as well as a real one.

Unicorns were not discussed again that evening, Suzy kept putting her finger to her lips frequently to remind Connie to keep their secret.

## Chapter 8

# The riding school

It was daytime again. The sky was pink and a rainbow was glowing brightly in the distance. Suzy found herself in the garden just outside the shed. She was alone. She looked through the shed window to see Horsey who was pawing the ground eager to get out.

She heard some footsteps behind her and turned round to see Dad and Connie approaching. Suzy was not sure if she was dreaming but decided to behave as if everything was real.

'Can *I* let her out this time?' she asked. Dad gave her the key.

'No, I want to let her out,' shouted Connie, trying to snatch the key off Suzy. They struggled finally ending up in a heap on the grass from which Suzy emerged victorious still holding the key. Before Connie could stand up she rushed over to open the shed door. Horsey jumped out neighing and shaking herself. Suzy stood still admiring the unicorn when she was suddenly knocked to the ground by Connie and another fight ensued.

'Stop it,' cried Dad, but they ignored him. Connie grabbed the key from Suzy and threw it over the fence into next door's garden.

'Girls stop!' said Dad. 'We won't be able to lock Horsey in the shed now.' The girls stood up glaring at each other.

'It was her fault,' said Connie.

'No it wasn't,' replied Suzy. 'You threw the key away.'

'I've an idea,' said Dad trying to calm things down. 'There's a horse riding school I found on the internet. It's not far from here. Let's see if they'll look after Horsey there.' Dad set off leading Horsey, after a while the girls followed him, excited to be going to the stables while still trying to look in a bad mood.

They passed the toy shop. It was open. They looked at the toys in the window. The monkey was still there but in place of the unicorn there was an ordinary brown pony. Dad stepped into the shop.

'Can I help you?' said the young man behind the counter.

'Is the lady who works here in today?'

The man looked at Dad with a puzzled expression.

'Have you got a unicorn in your garden?' Dad continued.

The man stood there shaking his head.

'I think you ought to leave sir,' he said.

Suzy and Connie looked up at Dad. Was he going to stand his ground, but no Dad turned around and walked out.

'We'll come back on Saturday,' he said to them.

Dad set off again as if he knew where he was going. Like before everyone they saw was accompanied by a unicorn. Suddenly they turned a corner and there straight ahead was a large sign, a unicorn on a pink background.

'What's that say?' asked Connie.

'It says Ruddington Unicorn Riding School,' replied Dad.

'Can we ride Horsey?' asked Suzy.

'Maybe,' said Dad. 'But first let's see if they can keep her in one of the stables.'

A man came up to them he was dressed in a blue

sleeveless jacket, jeans and long brown boots.

'Can I help you?' he said.

'Can you keep Horsey in a stable?' jumped in Connie.

'How much do you charge?' asked Dad.

'Normally there's a waiting list,' replied the man. 'But we have had a few of our unicorns change back into ponies. They have been returned to our other riding school so luckily we have some free stables today. We charge forty pounds a week if you look after its food and exercise it yourself or £150 if we look after all the unicorn's needs ourselves. If you let her be ridden by guests we will only charge £130 a week.'

'We need to think about it,' said Dad.

Dad and the girls sat in a ring around Horsey and began to think. Half an hour later they were still thinking. Dad broke the silence 'I think we could look after her ourselves.'

'So we could see Horsey every day,' said Suzy.

'We would have to,' said Dad.

'Hooray!' exclaimed Connie clapping her hands.

'We must be even more careful to keep our secret from Mum,' said Dad.

The girls both put their fingers to their lips.

'OK then,' said Dad.

He found the stable owner. 'We'll keep her here and look after her ourselves,' he said.

'Follow me,' said the man.

He led them over to the stables. There were four empty stables next to each other.

'You can choose which one you want,' he said.

Suzy pointed to the one that had pink curtains. 'Let's have that one,' she said.

They led Horsey into it and the unicorn seemed to smile. They patted her on the nose then closed the stable door. Dad followed the man into his office and paid him forty pounds.

'Dad,' said Suzy 'We haven't fed her today.'

'Can you feed him?' Dad asked the man.

' Sure, that will be another five pounds.'

Dad paid with a gloomy expression.

'And can I have your phone number,' asked the man. 'Just in case she doesn't settle.' Dad gave him the number.

They waved goodbye to Horsey. At that moment

Suzy woke up, she was in her bed. Outside it was just beginning to get light.

'Wake up you two,' said Mum. 'Rise and shine.'

## Chapter 9

# Dad investigates

The next two days followed a similar pattern. In the real daytime the girls went to school while in the pink daytime they found themselves at the Unicorn riding school, where they saw Horsey, cleaned her stable replacing the rabbit bedding, feeding her with Coco Pops, and taking her round the field. Suzy and Connie had tried to ride her but Horsey had shook her head and ran away when they tried to get on her back.

The next day, Thursday, Dad was supposed to be working at home. He thought he would use the time to do some detective work instead. After dropping the girls at school he set off for his first stop, the toy shop. He looked in the window and the monkey and Unicorn were still there. The brown pony had disappeared.

Dad strode into the shop determined to get some answers. The lady was behind the counter.

'Hello,' said Dad. 'Do you remember we took your unicorn to look after.'

'Of course I do,' she said.

'Well it's costing me a lot of money to look after her and I want to bring her back tomorrow.'

'But we agreed two weeks,' said the lady. 'You agreed. It's your responsibility to look after her.'

'If you don't take her back I'll report you to the police.'

'And what will you say? That I had a unicorn in my garden. I don't think they'll believe that.'

Dad was still angry but could see that she might be right. People like policemen didn't believe unicorns were real.

'Where did you get the unicorn from?' he asked.

'I didn't,' she said. She was just there one day I think she must have escaped. Then I started letting families look after her for a week or two as long as they paid me. What's wrong with that?'

'Well I'm bringing her back into the shop tomorrow anyway,' said Dad. And with that turned smartly and left the shop slamming the door behind him.

His next call was to the riding school. He followed the route as before till he reached the stables. He looked up at the sign it read Ruddington Pony Riding School. Instead of a unicorn there was a picture of a pony on a green background. Dad began to shiver he couldn't understand what was happening.

A man came over to him. He was older than the man he had spoken to in the pink daylight.

'What do you want?' he asked.

'I want to arrange to take my unicorn back home tomorrow morning.'

The man looked at him a frown on his face.

'Can you repeat that. I don't think I quite heard you.'

'I want to take my unicorn back tomorrow morning,' said Dad

'Look sir,' he said. There are no such animals as unicorns are you trying to be funny?'

'Let me show you,' said Dad. He walked over to the stable where Horsey was staying.

'There,' said Dad.

But when he looked inside there was only a pony contentedly drinking some water.

'What have you done with her,' said Dad indignantly. 'I'll report you to the police.'

'I think I should report *you*,' said the man and left Dad standing there.

Dad looked in the other stables all of which contained ponies, not a unicorn to be seen anywhere. He walked away thinking what to do next.

Dad's final stop was at the supermarket. Horsey had eaten nearly all the Coco Pops so Dad bought all the Coco Pops on the shelves, twenty packets and ten packets of Weetabix. Unfortunately it was yet again the same attendant who served him as last time.

'What's going on?' she asked looking at all the breakfast cereal packs.

'Oh you know, the children have such big appetites, they eat like horses.'

Dad still hadn't decided what to do, but he thought he must keep today's visits secret from the children. They would be so upset if they couldn't see Horsey.

However the next time it was daylight, pink daylight, everything was the same as before. Horsey was in the same stable pleased as always to see them.

# Chapter 10

## Mum finds out

It was Saturday and Dad had promised to buy the two animals from the toy shop, the monkey and the unicorn. The girls were ready to go. Mum was going to come with them and Dad was panicking. If the lady saw him or the girls she would ask about Horsey and Mum would find out about her. However Dad had got himself into many a scrape before and he had come up with a brilliant but simple idea. He would just pretend he had never spoken to the lady before and he would make Suzy and Connie keep quiet by giving them five pounds each.

They walked to the shop and went in. The lady nodded her head when she saw Dad and the girls.

'What is it this time?' she said in a bad tempered tone.

Dad and the girls said nothing, according to plan, so it was left to Mum to speak.

'We would like to buy the toy monkey and unicorn in

the window,' she said.

The lady picked them up and Mum paid for them.

'Don't forget to bring the unicorn back next week,' the lady said.

'Why should we do that?' asked Mum. 'It's ours now.'

'No it isn't,' said the lady. 'You agreed to bring her back.'

Mum was totally confused and looked across at Dad.

'Dave, what's going on?' she demanded.

'Let's go outside and I'll tell you,' he said.

'Well!' said Mum once they had left the shop.

'I can't tell you it's a secret,' tried Dad.

But Mum just gave him a fierce look. It was no good he would have to tell her the whole story. But Mum found it difficult to believe what he told her.

'Let's go through this again,' she said. 'You bought a live unicorn from the shop, even though there are no such things as unicorns. Then you kept this imaginary animal in our shed and fed it on Coco Pops.' Dad and the girls nodded.

'And then you took her to a unicorn stables that also doesn't exist except when you're dreaming, and you are paying the stables forty pounds in real money to look after her, and now the lady at the shop wants her back even though she only exists when you are dreaming and as I said unicorns aren't real anyway. And what's more you thought you could keep it a secret from me.'

'That's good,' said Dad. 'I can see you understand now.'

'Understand!' shouted Mum. 'Understand! I can't understand any of it.'

People in the street had begun to look at them as the noise got louder, and the girls covered up their ears.

'All right,' said Mum 'Show me the unicorn. Show me it now.'

'I can't,' said Dad rather weakly. 'But it looks a bit like the toy one we just bought.'

Mum gave him another fierce look raising an eyebrow.

'I can show you tonight if you join our dream, but I'm not sure if you will be able to if you don't believe in unicorns.'

'Well let's hope I can, otherwise you are in big trouble,' Mum said.

'Can we have our five pounds now?' asked Suzy. Mum

looked at Dad again and mouthed a word which Suzy thought might have been, useless. Dad gave the girls the money hoping that Mum wouldn't say anything.

# Chapter 11

# The pink daylight again

Dad was not feeling happy. He had tried so hard to look after Horsey and keep her comfortable and now he was in trouble because Mum did not believe in unicorns.

He had shown Mum all the packets of Coco Pops and Weetabix to back up his story, but Mum didn't think this was so unusual considering previous projects that Dad had started. The most likely explanation was that he had made up a story so the girls would not be disappointed when they didn't have enough money to buy the toy animals they wanted.

'She *is* real and unicorns *do* exist,' said Suzy. But Mum could not be persuaded.

'Why can't we go to see her at the stables?' Suzy asked Dad.

'Because she's only there in the pink daylight,' he replied.

'In the pink daylight,' echoed Connie.

Just then Dad had a new and he hoped good idea. They would all see Horsey tonight even if Mum didn't believe him. Dad explained.

'We'll all go to bed at the same time tonight, and I'll tie us together wrist to wrist. Then Mum will be dragged along into the pink daylight.'

Mum thought this was crazy, but she thought it might help Dad to see that his story could not be true. 'OK,' she said.

At eight o'clock they all got into Mum and Dad's bed. Dad having previously placed the cereal packs and rabbit bedding at the foot of the bed. Dad then tied all their wrists together and they all closed their eyes and tried to get to sleep.

The sky was pink and a rainbow appeared in the distance they were at the entrance to the Unicorn Riding School. Mum, Dad, Suzy and Connie still with their wrists bound together. This was a new experience for Mum, she didn't know if she was having a dream on her own. Dad undid the knots round their wrists, and gathered the breakfast cereals into his arms.

'See, the Unicorn Riding School,' he said pointing to the sign.

Mum nodded. Connie and Suzy skipped along to the stables. Mum looked in surprise to see a Unicorn in each one. They stopped outside the stable where Horsey was neighing excitedly.

'There's Horsey,' shouted Connie.

Mum nodded again.

Suzy let Horsey out and the girls chased her round the field meanwhile Dad changed the bedding and left the cereals in a corner of the stable.

Mum looked on in a daze, was she in a dream of her own, in the same dream as everyone else, or was this all real? She joined in chasing Horsey round the field and then something fantastic happened. Horsey came to a halt next to Mum.

'You can try to ride her,' said Suzy. 'She won't let me.'

Dad helped Mum to get on Horsey and then away she went first at a slow trot and then at a fast gallop. The girls cheered as Mum rode around clinging on to Horsey's mane. After a few minutes Horsey stopped and Dad and the girls helped Mum off.

'Now do you believe she's real?' asked Dad. 'I don't know whether any of this is real,' answered Mum. 'But I've had a wonderful time.'

Horsey trotted back to her stable and settled down to eat her way through the boxes of Coco Pops.

Suddenly Mum was back in bed. She looked across at the clock, it was seven o'clock in the morning. She noticed she was no longer tied to the children, and the breakfast cereal had disappeared. Dad and the girls were still asleep. She looked out of the window it was a grey, cloudy day. This, she was sure, was real.

# Chapter 12

# Horsey returned

The next few nights followed in a similar way. Mum though was starting to believe in unicorns or at least that they existed in the pink daylight. The time had come when the unicorn must be returned to the lady in the toy shop. Suzy and Connie knew they were going to have to return her one day but were very upset nonetheless.

They were at the Unicorn Riding School on Horsey's last day there. The sky was its usual pink colour the sun shining brightly and a rainbow as always in the distance.

Suzy and Connie patted Horsey to keep her calm while Dad slipped the reins onto her. They waved goodbye to the other unicorns and set off home Mum leading Horsey. They passed people walking to and fro all accompanied by their unicorns.

'Are we taking her to the shop?' Suzy asked.

Dad didn't reply straightaway, 'I'm not sure. If we take

her now , in the pink daylight, the lady won't be there.
There is a man who looks after the shop then and he
doesn't know anything about the unicorn. So I think we
will have to wait till the real morning, you know, when
we have woken up again. What do you think?'

They all tried to understand what Dad had said.
Connie tried especially hard and walked straight into a
lamp post, everyone else burst out laughing. 'That was
your fault Dad,' shouted Connie.

'Come here,' said Mum. 'Let me rub your head better.'

'Go away,' said Connie marching away in front of the
others swinging her arms as high as they would go.

'Well?' asked Dad.

'Well what?' Mum replied.

'Do you agree we don't take her to the shop?'

'Can you explain again,' Mum said.

Dad sighed. 'Look, we can't take the unicorn to the
shop because we have to hand her over to the lady and
she won't be there until the real morning.'

Suzy joined in 'Can we take her home to keep her for
a bit longer?'

'Yes I think that's what we'll have to do, but we must

take her back later.'

Suzy tried to hold back her tears. 'I suppose so,' she said.

When they got home Dad got the key for the shed opened the door and then tried to lead Horsey in. Horsey however had different ideas she was used to the comfortable stable now and had no intention of going back into the shed. They all got behind Horsey and tried to shove her in but it was no good. In the end Dad tied her reins to a branch.

Suzy woke up they were all in Mum and Dad's bed. She stretched her arms up and then screamed at the shock of seeing Horsey at the foot of the bed. This woke everyone else up and they all stared at the unicorn in their bedroom.

'I thought you left her tied up outside,' said Mum.

'I did,' said Dad. 'But that was in the dream, I don't know why she's inside'.

'Well let's get her outside now,' Mum said.

While saying this she suddenly realised this was the first time she had seen a unicorn in real daylight and then for the first time she believed unicorns were real and that Dad's story was true.

'I'm so sorry I didn't believe you,' she said.

Dad was so happy that he had been forgiven. He jumped out of bed and took Horsey into the garden where he tied her to the same branch as before. Then practising a few cartwheels he returned inside and ran up the stairs two at a time.

'When must we take Horsey back?' asked Suzy.

'We have to wait until it's dark so that no one can see her. Remember if she's discovered by the police she'll be taken away to a zoo.'

The rest of the day Suzy and Connie played with Horsey, making plaits in her hair, cooking some cupcakes for her, brushing her coat, and taking her for walks round the garden.

When it became dark, they put on Horsey's coat so that only her nose and eyes were visible and then Mum and Dad joined them to walk to the shop. Suzy led Horsey by the reins, no one spoke, their mood was sombre, they didn't want to take her back but they had promised.

The shop was closed, a dim light was on inside. Dad

knocked quietly on the door. 'We've brought the unicorn back,' he whispered through the letter box.

The lady took the cover off Horsey and examined her as if she was checking for scratches or bruises.

'Thank you,' she said. 'Goodnight.'

'Can we keep her a bit longer?' pleaded Connie.

'No,' said the lady. They waited for an explanation but the lady had already turned her back to them as she led Horsey into the back garden. Horsey let out a sad neigh but followed her.

They trudged back home Suzy and Connie letting out a painful sob every so often. When they got home Mum got out some chocolate biscuits for Suzy and Connie but they were too upset to eat what would normally have been a very special treat.

Dad led them up to bed.

'Can we get another Unicorn?' asked Suzy.

Dad didn't want to upset them anymore.

'We'll see.'

Maybe he could come up with one of his clever plans.

Chapter 13

# Dad makes some plans

Later that night Dad started working out his plan. He sat down at the kitchen table, a blank piece of paper in front of him. He wrote down Idea one, underlined it and then sat back to think. Dad usually had lots of ideas, not many of them sensible, but plenty of them. This time though he was struggling. He walked round and round the kitchen then sat down and started to write.

Idea one – Buy a unicorn.

Dad didn't bother thinking how to do this just yet.

Idea two – Buy a pony and turn it into a unicorn with a magic spell.

Idea three – Steal Horsey from the Toy Shop.

Dad was proud of coming up with these three very sensible ideas. He went into the living room where Mum was watching TV. He showed her the ideas. Mum sighed, to her eyes none of these ideas looked any good.

She went through them in a logical way one by one.

'Buying a unicorn. Where would you buy one from? I've only ever seen one unicorn, Horsey. Apart from her they don't exist.'

Dad shrugged his shoulders, 'OK, he admitted, not such a great idea.'

Mum continued 'Buy a pony and turn it into a unicorn with a magic spell. We could buy a pony, but magic isn't real.'

'It might be,' said Dad.

'But it isn't,' Mum said. 'Suzy might be happy with a pony though. We'll keep that idea in, without the magic spell.'

Dad nodded in agreement, but still hoped he could find a magic spell.

'Your last idea,' said Mum. 'We steal Horsey from the toy shop. Could we manage to do that without being caught?'

'Why not? We could go very late when everyone is asleep.'

'I don't know,' said Mum. 'If we get caught by the police then Horsey would get taken to the zoo and we could be put in prison.'

'We could risk it,' said Dad

'No,' said Mum. 'There is no way we are doing that, no way.'

Strangely enough Dad didn't nod his head to agree this time.

'So we'll buy a pony tomorrow,' said Mum.

Dad smiled.

Next morning at breakfast Suzy was playing with her new unicorn toy, eating a bowl of Coco Pops while pretending to feed it. Connie was drawing a picture of a unicorn.

Mum explained what they were going to do. 'We can't get you a unicorn,' she said looking at Suzy. 'But we can buy a pony instead. You'll still be able to look after it and you can learn how to ride it.'

'But Dad said I could have a unicorn, a pony wouldn't be the same.'

'It would be almost the same,' replied Mum.

'It wouldn't be as beautiful,' said Suzy.

'I want a unicorn too,' said Connie.

'I can change the pony into a unicorn with a magic spell,' said Dad.

He ignored Mum's look.

Chapter 14

# The magic spell

The next morning the Goodwin household woke up.
They had all had a really good night's sleep, no one
had dreamt of unicorns in the pink daylight. Dad had
made his plan to find a magic spell, he decided not to
tell anyone else, especially Mum, as he knew she didn't
believe in magic.

Instead of going straight into work he took a detour
into the village, his destination the village library. He
walked in and without stopping to talk to the librarian
went straight over to the magic section. There were
books explaining card tricks, tricks with coins, tricks
with string, how to saw someone in half (he made a note
to come back to that later) but nothing on changing
ponies to unicorns.

He thought of asking the librarian for help, but then
he remembered his previous conversations with her

about the book that kept disappearing and reappearing, so he decided not to.

On his way out of the library he paused in front of the notice board. There was a notice there in very small writing. Unicorns Anonymous. Do you think you're seeing unicorns visit our unicorn discussion group we meet every Monday midday at 13, Carter View, Ruddington. Only people who believe in magic are welcome.

Dad could just get there in time. He found the house quickly and looked up at it. It was just an ordinary looking house, white doors and window frames, and a small garden, there were no signs of unicorns anywhere.

He knocked on the door, an elderly lady opened it.

'Is this the right place for Unicorns Anonymous?' he asked rather nervously.

'Do you believe in magic?' asked the lady.

'I certainly do,' Dad replied.

'OK it *is* the right place, come on in,' she said.

Somehow Dad didn't think he had been given a very thorough check. He walked into the living room and sat down on a sofa. He looked around him, apart from the lady there were 5 other men. Perhaps only men believe in magic he thought. Two of the men were wearing masks that looked like they had been cut out from the back of cereal packets. Dad didn't recognise anyone.

'We've got a new member today,' the lady said 'Can you introduce yourself and tell us why you've come.'

Dad went through the whole story of how he had bought Horsey, kept her in the shed, looked after her in the pink daylight and then returned her to the toy shop. He said that he had come to the group to find a magic spell to turn a pony into a unicorn.

'I think we should all introduce ourselves first,' said the Lady. 'I'm Carol.'

Three of the men introduced themselves as Tom, Mark, and Bobby the two masked men went by the names of Squirrel and Badger.

'Who wants to comment on what David said, 'Carol asked.

After a long pause Squirrel started 'I've only ever seen unicorns from a long distance away, they could just be white ponies, and I've never tried to change them with a magic spell.'

Dad didn't believe that Squirrel had ever seen a unicorn.

Next it was Tom. 'As you all know I am the only person who has photos of a real unicorn.'

Carol interrupted, 'We don't all agree,' she said. 'It looked a bit like you had stuck a cardboard horn on a pony's head.'

'That's a lie,' replied Tom crossly.

'Well why wasn't it there when you took a photo on a windy day?' asked Badger.

'That's because the horn sometimes goes very small to protect it from the cold.'

This was greeted by a low murmuring amongst the others with a great deal of head shaking.

'Has anyone heard about the magic spell David is looking for?' Carol asked.

'I know a spell to change a caterpillar into a butterfly,' Squirrel stated.

'You don't need a spell for that you idiot,' said Bobby.

'Don't you call me an idiot,' shouted Squirrel. 'Who was it thought they saw a unicorn and it turned out to be a goat.'

'Let's have some tea and biscuits,' suggested Carol in

an attempt to calm things down.

Dad stayed for the refreshments but the more he heard them chatting the more he was convinced that only he had seen a real unicorn. Nobody had heard of a spell to change a pony into a unicorn. What's more he thought they were all a bit stupid.

Dad decided he wouldn't go to another meeting of Unicorns Anonymous, ever.

He went into work spending a lot of time thinking how he could persuade Mum to steal the unicorn from the toy shop.

# Chapter 15

# Dad gets his way

Meanwhile Mum had been following her plan to buy a pony. She had checked on the computer but all the ponies for sale cost at least five thousand pounds, except for one that was only three hundred pounds. When she phoned the owner for more details she found out it only had three legs. She didn't think Suzy or Connie would want one with less than four legs. When Dad came back from work with the girls she still hadn't decided what to do. When the children had settled down to watch yet another episode of Peppa Pig she started a conversation with Dad.

'You know I was going to buy a pony.'

'Yes.'

'Well it's a bit more expensive than I realised, guess how much?'

Dad thought of a figure that would be higher than Mum had found.

'Five hundred pounds?'

'Not even close,' said Mum. 'The cheapest was £5,000'
(She thought it best not to mention the three legged one
in case Dad went for that, he always had an eye for a
bargain).

'Wow!' Dad gasped. 'I don't think we could afford that.'

At the same time he saw his opportunity to put his
own plan into action.

'Even if we did buy it I don't think we could change it
into a unicorn with a magic spell.'

'I thought you agreed we couldn't do that last night,'
said Mum.

'I did, but now I'm more certain it's not a good idea.'

'Why?' asked Mum

Dad told her about his trip to the library to find a
magic spell but didn't mention his visit to Unicorns
Anonymous in case this started off a long conversation.
Instead he put forward his idea that he had had all along.

'The only thing we can do is to steal Horsey from the
toy shop.'

'No, I said we could never do that,' said Mum.

'Well *you* wouldn't have to' said Dad. 'I could do it

with the girls.'

'And what would happen if you got caught?'

'I don't think the lady at the shop would report us, after all she may have stolen it herself, and in any case I don't think there is any law about stealing unicorns.'

Mum could see a few flaws in Dad's plan but what was worse , putting up with the girls moaning about not having a unicorn for the next six months or having Dad put into prison . It didn't take her long to decide.

'OK we'll risk you going to prison. But if you get caught I'll say I know nothing about it.'

Dad was not too pleased with Mum's attitude, but he had got permission to carry out his plan, which was all that mattered.

At bed time the girls asked when they would get their unicorn. Dad didn't want to tell them about stealing Horsey in case they got too excited and started telling all their school friends. He tapped the side of his nose mysteriously and just said 'Wait till tomorrow night, now have a good sleep.'

Suzy was sure that Dad had once again come up with a brilliant idea and everything would be fine.

# Chapter 16

# Dad's brilliant plan

'Suzy Goodwin, what's five take away two?'

'Ugh!' said Suzy who had just been daydreaming about riding on her unicorn.

'Well?'

Suzy imagined five unicorns in a field then two of them being chased away by a dog.

'Three,' she replied.

'Very Good,' said Mrs Smith. 'But please try to stay awake.'

Suzy looked at the clock there was just ten minutes until the class finished, and until Dad would collect her and Connie. The minutes passed by very very slowly, but at last school was finished for the day. Dad was waiting for them in the playground.

'Are we getting the unicorn now?' asked Connie.

'It's too light at the moment,' said Dad. 'You need to

have your tea and then get changed.'

Suzy wondered why they had to get changed but didn't question Dad.

It was difficult to eat, they were both so excited. They ate as little as possible and then ran upstairs to get changed. Dad had told them to wear their darkest tops and dark trousers and black coats. He came up to check.

'That looks all right,' he said. 'Stand still while I put this on.'

He dabbed a cloth into a tin of black shoe polish and applied it to their cheeks and forehead.

'There, that should do,' he said. No one will be able to see us now.'

'This is what we're going to do,' said Dad. 'As soon as it gets dark, we're walking to the toy shop. I'm going to climb over the garden fence using our stepladder, tie a rope round Horsey's head then lead her up and over the fence using two ramps I made at work. We're going to lead her back to our house and then keep her hidden in the shed until I think what to do next.'

'Yippee!' shouted Connie. 'We're going to have Horsey back.'

Suzy didn't want to get too excited until Horsey was back in the shed, she had seen some of Dad's plans go wrong in the past.

They waved goodbye to Mum and set off. Suzy and Connie were each carrying a wooden ramp. Dad had a step ladder and an axe. They had to stop to have a rest every few minutes and in the end Dad ended up having to carry everything.

It was dark when they reached the shop with thankfully no moonlight. Dad put the stepladder by the fence to the back garden.

'I'm just going to see if Horsey is here,' he said as he climbed the stepladder.

'Yes she is,' he said. 'Pass me the ramp.'

Suzy and Connie struggled to lift the ramp up and Dad laid it against the fence inside the garden.

'Now put the other ramp against the fence.'

The girls tried their best but they had run out of strength so Dad had to climb down the ladder and help them. He picked up the axe then climbed up the ladder and jumped off the top into the garden. He felt in his pocket for the rope and put it round Horsey's neck.

'I'm going to push her over the ramp, then when she comes down the other ramp you have to stop her from running away.'

He led her over to the bottom of the ramp and then got behind her and tried to push her up. Horsey started to neigh and refused to move.

'I need your help,' he said. 'Climb up the step ladder and I'll let you down.'

They followed dad's instructions.

'Now,' said Dad. 'Get behind her and when I say go we'll all push together to get her up the ramp.'

'Go!'

But it was no good they couldn't move Horsey.

'Right,' said Dad. 'Stand to the side.'

The girls moved and watched in amazement as Dad attacked the fence with the axe making a unicorn sized hole in a fence panel. Then before they could react Horsey sped past them through the hole and disappeared off into the night.

'Quick after her!' shouted Dad, picking up the ladder and the axe and starting to run after the unicorn. But it was too late Horsey had disappeared.

The three of them trudged home hoping that Horsey had gone there, but she hadn't.

'We'll have to look for her tomorrow,' said Dad.

Mum tried to console them making some hot milk and letting them go to bed without scrubbing the shoe polish off their faces. Suzy hugged and stroked her toy unicorn, but it just wasn't the same as the real one.

# Chapter 17

## The RSPCA

Suzy and Connie woke up the following morning. They had hoped it would be pink daylight but it was just a rather dull grey sky. They looked out of their bedroom window, no sign of a unicorn in the garden. This was the worst morning they could remember.

Dad had explained to Mum what had happened.

'We have to find her today,' said Connie.

'We can try the Riding School first,' said Suzy.

'Yes, but she's only been there in the pink daylight, still that's probably the best place to start,' said Dad.

'First you two need to have a bath and get this shoe polish off,' said Mum.

While they went to the bathroom, there was a loud knock at the door. Dad went to open it the lady from the shop was standing there.

'It was you wasn't it?' she blurted out.

'Good morning,' said Dad coolly. 'Can I help you?'

'Yes you jolly well can, you can return my unicorn straightaway and pay for my fence to be mended.'

'I don't know what you're talking about,' said Dad. 'We haven't got a unicorn here you can look in our garden if you like'.

'OK,' said the lady. 'Show me.'

Dad led her down the side of the house into the back garden. The lady had a good look round but had to admit there was nothing there.

'I still think it was you,' she said angrily. 'In fact I know it was. You haven't heard the last of this. And don't you dare come to my shop again'

'Well if you're convinced it was me, report it to the police.'

'I did but when I mentioned the word unicorn they rang off.'

'Well in that case, goodbye,' said Dad, who was relieved when the lady walked off grumbling to herself.

Half an hour later the family were in the car driving to the Riding School. Mum parked the car by the office. 'Let me do the talking,' she said.

She went into the office and spoke to the man behind the counter. 'Our pony escaped last night and we thought she might have come here.'

'I'll ask one of our stable lads.'

He went off in the direction of the stables.

'But it's a unicorn, not a pony,' said Suzy.

'I know, but not everyone believes in unicorns, I didn't used to.'

They waited for what seemed a long time for the man to return.

'The lads haven't seen any stray ponies but one suggested you try the RSPCA someone might have taken yours there.'

'Where is that?' said Mum.

'It's on Richmond Street just opposite the garage.'

'Thanks for your help,' said Mum.

'What's the RCA?' asked Connie .

'The RSPCA,' said Dad. 'It's where they keep animals that have been neglected by their owners and sometimes people who find strays take them there to be looked after.'

They set out for the RSPCA soon finding it. It

consisted of a large grassy area with several concrete
buildings and a number of barns. There were some
outside pens with goats in them and one with an old
donkey. Mum walked into the building which had a sign
that read Reception.

A young lady was sitting at a desk. Mum repeated the
story she had told at the Riding School. The lady looked
curiously at Mum. 'What did it look like?' she asked.

'It's mainly white with a pink mane,' said Mum.

'Follow me,' the lady said.

They all followed her to a huge barn in the far corner
of a field.

'Only one of you can come in here and you have to
sign this document first,' the lady said pulling a sheet of
paper from her back pocket. 'It will have to be an adult.'

'You go,' said Mum to Dad.

Dad read through the sheet of paper. It read:-

RSPCA – U section

I hereby promise that I will not reveal what I see in
this section to any person without permission of the
Ruddington RSPCA'.

There was a space for Dad to enter his name, address,

phone number and to add his signature.

'What happens if I break this promise?' Dad asked.

'Then we will decide on the punishment in our U section court,' said the lady.

Dad filled in the details and signed the document.

The lady tapped some numbers into a keypad on the door and walked in with Dad. They walked through a dark tunnel the lady leading with a torch. At the end of the tunnel there was another door with another keypad the lady again tapped in some numbers. The doors sprang open revealing a large grassy area lit up through a glass ceiling. Surrounding the grass were a number of stables , Dad counted about twenty. Dad looked into one a unicorn was eating some hay.

'Have a look at number ten,' the lady said. 'Is that yours?'

Dad looked in and there was Horsey drinking some water she neighed at him and Dad nodded.

'She was outside when one of our stable lads came in early this morning . He brought her inside before anyone else could see her. I can bring the rest of your family in now and you can walk her round here. We let them run round in the field outside but only when it is dark. We will look after her now but you can come to see her when you want. But I must get your wife to sign the document too and then take photos of all of you.'

Dad walked out of the barn, Mum signed the form and then they followed him into the barn. The lady opened the gate to stable ten and Horsey trotted out. The girls cried with joy at seeing Horsey. They took it in turns at leading her round.

After an hour it was time to go.

'She likes Coco Pops and Weetabix' Dad said.

'That's a bit unusual for unicorns' said the lady. 'But we'll get some to add to her other food.'

'Can we see her tomorrow?' asked Connie. 'You can see her anytime you want,' replied the lady.

They drove back home the girls singing made up unicorn songs. This was the best afternoon they could remember.

# Section X

The days and weeks passed. Suzy and Connie were so happy seeing Horsey nearly every day. They became friendly with the lady whose name they found was Anne. Then one day Anne suggested Suzy have another go at trying to ride Horsey. Suzy was quite nervous about it remembering that Horsey had only let Mum ride her before.

Anne put some reins and a saddle on Horsey then lifted Suzy up. At first nothing happened but then Horsey started to trot slowly. Suzy gradually got better and better at riding and after a few months was riding as well as Mum. Horsey still wouldn't let Connie ride her. Connie didn't mind too much as long as she could feed her and stroke her neck.

Then one day something changed. When Suzy, Connie, Mum and Dad went to see Horsey. Anne said she had some news for them and asked them to sit down on a sofa in the office. 'We've had to move Horsey into our X section,' she said.

'What's that?' asked Mum.

'I can't tell you unless you sign another form.'

'What, even Connie?' said Dad.

'I'm afraid so'

She gave Dad the form.

It read, I promise I will not tell anyone about what happens in section X , ever.

'Should we sign it?' asked Dad. 'It might be something bad that we need to report to the police.'

'Just sign it,' said Mum.

So Dad signed it, then Mum, then Suzy wrote her name down and finally Connie tried her best to write her name.

'Well, tell us,' said Dad.

Anne started in a low voice. 'Some of our unicorns change into ponies when they get older. We think Horsey might be changing. Her horn has got a bit smaller and her coat has turned a bit darker. We will keep her in another barn that we call section X to help her change. While she's there we change a few things. She has more pony type food to eat, so more grass and hay and gradually cutting down on Coco Pops and Weetabix. We introduce her to ponies at the Ruddington Pony Riding School to help her make friends there. We also organise a visit to the Pony School so she can see what the stables are like.

If after a few weeks she has completely turned into a pony we move her out there. However if she hasn't, then we will return her to our U section. I'm sure you've got a lot of questions so ask me anything you want to. It was silent except for the sound of Connie practising counting up to a hundred.

Then Suzy started 'Can we still see Horsey if she changes into a pony?'

'Yes you can, she will be at the Pony Riding School and you can still ride her.'

'But will she still know me?'

'She will remember everything about her life as a unicorn, she'll just look different.'

'How many unicorns change into ponies?' asked Mum.

'About half,' said Anne.

'Do any change into ponies and then change back?' said Mum.

'I haven't seen any that do that,' said Anne.

'Can we see her when she's in section X?' asked Suzy.

'It's best you don't to give her the best chance to adapt, I'll let you know when it's all right to see her again either as a unicorn or pony.'

They all got into the car and started off home. The girls were very upset.

'I don't want a pony,' said Connie.

'I don't either, I want Horsey to stay a unicorn,' said Suzy. 'But how can we stop her from changing.'

Dad tried to reassure them 'Anne said only half the unicorns change into ponies, so Horsey might not change.'

'But she might,' said Suzy.

'Well I've got a plan,' said Dad. 'We could steal her from Section X before she has had chance to change.'

'I don't think that would work,' said Mum. 'Even if you could get in she might run away again.'

'So what's *your* plan?' asked Dad.

'Could we see her at the RSPCA in the pink daylight?' asked Mum. 'Then we could feed her with lots of Coco Pops and Weetabix which might stop her changing.' This sounded more like one of Dad's plans than Mum's.

'We haven't had dreams like that since we took Horsey back to the toy shop' said Dad.

'I know,' said Mum. 'But why not?'

'Maybe she knew we weren't her owners anymore,' said Suzy.

'We're still not, Anne is her owner now,' said Mum.

'But we know someone who *does* own a unicorn,' said Dad. 'Jack's dad'.

# Chapter 19

# The sleepover

The next day. Dad and Connie went round to Jack's house. Dad knocked on the door and Mike, Jack's dad opened it.

'Hello,' said Dad. 'How are you?'

'Very well' said Mike.

'Connie says she wants to stay for a sleepover tonight.'

'I like sleepovers here,' said Connie. 'We can sleep in the tent in the garden.'

'Well no problem then,' said Mike. 'I'll just get Jack.'

Jack came rushing in from the living room and gave Connie a big hug.

'Let's go and put the tent up' he said.

While the children went into the garden Dad and Mike went into the kitchen to have a coffee.

'There's something I've been meaning to ask you,' said Dad.

'Go ahead.'

Dad paused and then came out with it 'Have you got a unicorn?'

'What makes you think that?' said Mike.

'I saw you with one in a dream,' said Dad, 'and you called out to me.'

'Well there you are then,' said Mike. 'It was just a dream.'

'No I don't think so,' said Dad. 'We had a unicorn and then it was in the dream that we all had.'

'This is very strange,' said Mike. 'We haven't got a unicorn but I have had some dreams when I have got a unicorn, and so has Jack. They started when we bought a toy unicorn from the toy shop. I did see you in one of our dreams but I didn't think it was real.'

'Is the sky pink when you have these dreams?' asked Dad.

'Yes , and there's always a rainbow.'

'Listen,' said Dad.' I want you to have a dream tonight where you wake up in pink daylight and to take Connie with you.'

'But I don't know how to make the dream happen,' said Mike.

'I think if you sleep in the tent with Jack and Connie and they both have their toy unicorns with them then it might work.'

'Well suppose it does, what then?' said Mike.

'I want you to go to the RSPCA and let Connie see our unicorn, Horsey. She'll know what to do.'

'Why do you want to go to the RSPCA?' asked Mike.

'I can't tell you,' said Dad remembering the promises he had made not to tell anyone about section U and X, 'but it is very important and I would be very grateful.'

'Will it be safe?' asked Mike.

'I'm sure it will be.'

'OK,' said Mike. 'Let's do it'

'Great,' said Dad. 'I'll bring Connie round, about seven.'

'Connie! Time to go now,' he shouted. 'We'll come back for your sleepover after tea.'

Connie waved goodbye to Jack and followed Dad out.

'Bye Mike,' said Dad. 'See you later'.

Later on after Connie had eaten her tea, Mum and Dad had to get her ready for her sleepover. Suzy wanted to go to as well and Mum and Dad said she could as long it was all right with Jack's mum and dad. They said it was, so Suzy and Connie got dressed in their pj's and coats ready to go.

Dad also got a bag of breakfast cereals to take. Two boxes of Coco Pops, one of Weetabix and a box of blueberry pieces. He also put Suzy's unicorn toy in the bag. Then he explained the plan.

'You will go to sleep holding the bag of cereals, then if you wake up in the pink daylight, follow Jack, his dad and their unicorn. They will take you to the RSPCA, where you will look for Horsey. If you find her give her all the cereals and make sure she eats them. That's all you need to do. That should stop her wanting to change into a pony.'

'What happens if we don't find her?' asked Suzy.

'We'll try another plan tomorrow,' said Dad.

They set off to Jack's house where Dad kissed them both and said goodnight.

# Chapter 20

# Finding Horsey

The sky was pink and a rainbow was glowing in the distance. Suzy, Connie, Jack and his dad were in the street outside Jack's home. Alongside them was a unicorn, she looked a bit like Horsey but a bit taller and her mane was gold instead of Horsey's pink.

The group set off for the RSPCA passing other people with Unicorns as they strode along. It was daytime but there were no cars on the road.

'What's your unicorn called?' Connie asked Jack.

'We call her Beauty,' said Jack. 'But I don't know her real name.'

'Does she let you ride her?' asked Suzy.

'We only see her in this dream,' explained Jack's dad, and then we only walk to the end of the road before we wake up, so we don't have a chance to practise riding her.

'I don't think it's a dream,' said Suzy.

They carried on in silence. When they reached the end of the road Suzy turned round to ask Jack's dad which way to turn . That was then she noticed that only Connie was there all the others had disappeared.

'We have to go on,' she said. 'I think it's this way,' she continued, pointing to the right.

Connie nodded.

After what seemed a long time Suzy spotted a sign with the letters RSPCA on it. They approached the sign and looked through the fence into the fields beyond. They walked up to the office, a friendly-looking man was behind the counter.

Suzy went up to him. 'Is Anne here?'

'We don't have anyone called Anne working here. Can I help?'

'We want to see our unicorn, she's called Horsey. Do you know where she is? She was in Section X.'

'There isn't a Section X,' the man said. 'All of our unicorns are exercising in the field near the row of trees. You can walk over there and ask one of the stable lads.'

'OK thank you,' said Suzy.

The sisters ran over to the row of trees. On the way

they passed some animals they had never seen before, some looked like pigs but with longer hind legs like a kangaroo, some goats that were twice as big as normal goats. There were also some ponies.

When they reached the field by the trees they could see about twenty unicorns galloping round. They couldn't though see Horsey amongst them.

One of the stable lads was standing watching. Suzy approached him.

'We've come to see Horsey. Is she here?' she asked.

'Yes I'll get her.'

He whistled loudly in the direction of another stable lad, who wandered over.

'Can you fetch Horsey over here?' he asked.

The other stable lad went and grabbed the reins on one of the unicorns slowing it down and brought it over.

At first Suzy and Connie didn't recognize her. Her coat had changed into a light brown colour, her mane was white and her horn had become very small. But then she neighed and they recognized her voice.

Connie opened her bag and then she noticed something wrong. This wasn't the bag with the breakfast cereals in it, this one had the snacks to eat at night two bars of white chocolate and two bags of crisps.

'What shall I do?' she asked Suzy.

Suzy thought hard. She didn't want to make the long walk back to Jack's home to fetch the other bag.

'Take the wrappers off the chocolate bag and open the crisp packets then put the bag over her nose,' she said.

'But we won't have anything to eat at night,' said Connie.

'You have to do it,' said Suzy. 'Else Horsey will change into a pony.'

Connie put the bag over Horsey's nose. The unicorn gobbled up all the food very quickly.

'Do you think she's changing back ?' said Connie.

But when Suzie looked the unicorn had disappeared , they were back in the tent in Jack's garden. It was early morning the sky outside was a light blue colour.

# Chapter 21

# Horsey Today

It is now a year after that sleepover. Horsey is still a unicorn and her horn has grown back. Her coat is white and her mane pink. She is no longer in section X having been returned to section U a few weeks after the sleepover. Dad has paid the toy-shop lady for the repairs to the fence and the girls are now allowed to go back into the shop.

The girls see Horsey every week and they can now ride her. Their dreams of the pink daylight have stopped.

Most people still don't believe unicorns are real.


THE END